Layla settled on the one decision she had to make for everyone involved, including herself. "I'm staying to help find the dress."

"Are you sure? I got the impression you weren't planning to be here very long."

"I can stay." The skepticism in Bastian's eyes pulled out an excuse. "I'm between places in my life right now. I'm taking time to figure things out."

Where had that come from? She was burned out and needed some time by the ocean. But why did the figuring-things-out part feel so...legitimate?

Bastian reached across the table and took her hand. "I understand what you're saying. I'm in the process of figuring things out, too. So it's settled. Well, almost settled." He chuckled wryly. "I'm glad you were here to help."

The sincerity in his eyes drove Layla's gaze down to their joined hands.

He said that now. But would Bastian feel the same way when he found out she was Ruby's granddaughter?

Dear Reader,

Welcome to Buttons & Lace Boutique, located in the heart of Bolan, Maryland. As the sign just outside town says, Friends and Smiles for Miles Live Here. If you've visited before, it's good to see you again!

While you're here, you'll get a chance to catch up with the Tillbridge family and other friends you've met in the Tillbridge Stables series. And you'll have the opportunity to meet our new arrivals—Layla Price and Sebastian "Bastian" Raynes in *The Designer's Secret*, Small Town Secrets book two.

In this story, Layla is delivering a curse-breaking payoff. It's the only logical solution to resolve her grandmother's decades-old problem with a former friend and business partner. Bastian is at a place in his life of figuring out what's next. Their journeys lead them to each other and the small town where everyone there, and two counties over, knows everybody's business.

But with Layla and Bastian, secrets are held close. Promises are kept. Passion is unleashed. And important truths are discovered. One important four-letter *L* word is the key to everything.

I hope Layla and Bastian's story makes you smile as you read about how they reach their destination. Hearing from readers is something that adds a smile to my day. Instagram, Facebook and my newsletter are three of my favorite places to connect. I look forward to meeting you there. You can find out more about me, the upcoming books in the Small Town Secrets series, as well as the connected books in the Tillbridge Stables series, at ninacrespo.com.

Wishing you all the best and happy reading!

Nina

The Designer's Secret

NINA CRESPO

HARLEQUIN

SPECIAL
EDITION

HARLEQUIN®
SPECIAL EDITION™

ISBN-13: 978-1-335-72415-1

The Designer's Secret

Copyright © 2022 by Nina Crespo

For questions and comments about the quality of this book, please contact us at CustomerService@Harlequin.com.

Harlequin Enterprises ULC
22 Adelaide St. West, 41st Floor
Toronto, Ontario M5H 4E3, Canada
www.Harlequin.com

Printed in U.S.A.

Recycling programs for this product may not exist in your area.

Nina Crespo lives in Florida, where she indulges in her favorite passions—the beach, a good glass of wine, date night with her own real-life hero and dancing. Her lifelong addiction to romance began in her teens while on a "borrowing spree" In her older sister's bedroom, where she discovered her first romance novel. Let Nina's sensual contemporary stories feed your own addiction for love, romance and happily-ever-after. Visit her at ninacrespo.com.

Books by Nina Crespo

Harlequin Special Edition

Small Town Secrets

The Chef's Kiss

Tillbridge Stables

The Cowboy's Claim
Her Sweet Temptation
The Cowgirl's Surprise Match

Visit the Author Profile page
at Harlequin.com for more titles.

To my real-life hero and best friend,
thank you for being by my side.
A long-overdue shout-out to
Nadine Nagamatsu for helping bring the
Tillbridge Stables and Small Town Secrets series
to life. Denny S. Bryce, Michele Arris, Mia Sosa,
Tracey Livesay, Tif Marcelo, Priscilla Oliveras—
you are still beyond fabulous! Cathy Yardley, there
are not enough words to express my appreciation
for you. Megan Broderick, thank you for your
patience, understanding and guidance with every
book. And a huge thank-you to all of my readers.
I hope this book brings you an enjoyable escape
as you turn the pages. And as always, my gratitude
to Life, Breath and Inspiration for providing
the light and leading the way.

Chapter One

Layla Price downed vitamins with her coffee, trying to wake up. She'd only been at her desk a couple of hours, but her brain had already gone numb from staring at the multiple rows of numbers on the computer screen.

I hate spreadsheets.

As an accountant, that probably wasn't the Monday-morning pep talk she should give herself. Of course she appreciated the detailed organization of the document in front of her. She just needed to concentrate.

Long minutes later, the restlessness she'd been battling for the past eight months crept farther in, trapping her in a sensation that she needed to escape.

Three more days...

That's how long she had until she could recharge and get past whatever this was—sleep deprivation, a slight case of burnout, not enough sun. Lack of vitamin D affected motivation, didn't it?

After inputting the wrong number for the third time, Layla released her dark curls from her ponytail and slumped back in the chair. She would agree that two plus two equaled five if it meant she could leave her office now for her two-week vacation.

Giving in to her wandering mind, the blue-white-and-gold abstract mural on the wall in front of her morphed into the perfect ocean view.

She closed her eyes, envisioning herself in her favorite orange bathing suit instead of her olive-colored dress.

The sun shining through the tinted glass windows in her third-floor office became warm unfiltered light beaming down from a cloudless sky. As she slipped off her red-soled black pumps and curled her toes into the light beige carpet, it was as if she could feel the sand caving around her toes. The cool air blowing from the vent above her desk changed into a gentle breeze.

No deadlines to meet, budgets to assess or bad client decisions to fix. Just bliss.

A muffled buzzing replaced the symphony of the imagined ocean waves, and the daydream dissipated.

Layla sat straight in the chair and followed the sound to her phone underneath a stack of papers in front of her.

A text from her younger sister, Tyler, lit up the screen.

Are you busy?

As Layla tapped in a response, sarcasm tinged a quiet laugh.

Yes.

The answer to that question should have been obvious. Tyler had emailed her a budget report late last night. And asked her to put a rush on reviewing it.

Tyler helped manage Sashay Chic as creative director, along with their stepmother, Patrice, who was the head of their family's retail clothing company.

Some days it felt as if her sister thought she and Sashay Chic Apparel were her only accounting clients.

Dots floated in a message bubble and Tyler's reply appeared.

I'm in the elevator. On my way up.

Seriously? *Nooo.* She loved Tyler, but she had a ton of things to do before temporarily handing over the reins of her business to Naomi, a semi-retired accountant who helped out whenever Layla was out of her office.

A knock sounded at the door and Tyler strode in. Runway model perfect in a fitted burgundy pantsuit, the thumps of her blush-colored stilettos echoed as she executed a *Top Model* walk that would have earned her a Tyra Banks arched brow of approval.

Straight shoulder-length black hair and flawlessly applied makeup complemented her deep brown complexion. Her honey-brown eyes—a family trait Layla and Tyler had inherited from their mother's side of the family—were framed by long lashes. A matte red lipstick highlighted her mouth. The color would have looked even more striking if she hadn't been frowning.

Tyler dropped her purse in one of the twin teal chairs in front of the desk. "That shade of olive washes you out, and your lipstick is too pale. You need to wear a shade of plum that pops."

"It's good to see you, too." Layla flashed an overly bright smile. "And thanks for dropping by to tell me I look like crap."

"That's not what I said." Genuine caring and exasperation reflected on Tyler's face. "All you need to do is pull your hair up into a messy bun, wrap a colorful scarf around your neck and freshen your makeup."

"Sure thing. I'll do that right after I finish reviewing the report you dropped into my inbox over the weekend. And if you're here to bug me about it, you can walk your cute butt back out the door."

"As much as I would like your stamp of approval on the budget, that's not why I'm here. I have bigger problems." Tyler paced near the desk. "Patrice postponed my fashion collection debut for Sashay Chic, indefinitely. And she says at next month's quarterly meeting, the board won't approve my proposal to revive our fashion shows or participate in the celebration of Atlanta Fashion Week."

"That's a lot. What happened?"

"I have no idea. I just know Grandma Ruby is behind it. She's turned against me and persuaded everyone to go along with her."

Layla sat back in the chair. "Grandma's turned against you? That doesn't sound right."

"I know." Tyler threw up her hands. "None of it makes sense. Before Grandma went to Nevada last week, she was excited about what I'd planned, especially the idea of paying homage to some of her past designs."

"Did she give a reason why she changed her mind?"

"She told Patrice now isn't the time for the company to go through a drastic transformation. But the pieces I've designed don't come close to drastic. And before Grandma retired from running the company, she had seasonal fashion shows for Sashay Chic featuring new signature designs."

"I think the collection you've created is perfect."

Versatile pieces that could go from day to night were what a lot of people would love to have in their closets. There had to be something else in the mix.

"What's Dad and Patrice's take on it?"

Tyler breathed out a chuckle. "You know how Dad is. He's always deep in corporate-attorney mode. He said negotiate with Grandma. Patrice recommended I don't. She said Grandma and I are equally passionate about our positions on this, and that if I tried to talk to her, our conversation wouldn't go anywhere because we're too much alike."

Alike? Tyler was an exact younger copy of Grandma Ruby, from her face to her talent, all the way down to her stubborn streak. And Patrice was right—if the two women tried to talk about it, their conversation wouldn't go anywhere but sideways. Once Tyler or their grandmother believed in something, it was difficult to convince them to see things differently.

Layla saved the document on the screen. "You could pull the proposal from the board's agenda before it's voted on and introduce it next quarter. That way, Grandma will have time to settle down, and you'll have time to find out what her concerns are and address them. Once you do, I'm sure she'll be good with everything."

"But we don't have the luxury of time." Tyler partially sat on the side of the desk. "You've seen the financials. Sales are declining because we're losing our competitive edge. We need a strong signature line of original designs that will recapture the attention of our customers and attract new ones. This collection—it's the best I've created. It would be a huge success in our physical stores and online. I can feel it. But because of Grandma, my work might not see the light of day. And I can't do anything about it."

"I wish I had the magic answer, but I don't." Layla got up and sat next to Tyler. She wrapped an arm around her. "I'm sorry this is happening to you."

"It's not your fault. It's mine." Hurt and frustration

pooled in Tyler's eyes. "I should have asked more questions eight months ago before I left New York and accepted this job. But I was so excited the opportunity finally happened. Becoming an executive at Sashay Chic and debuting my own collection at our stores has been my biggest dream. I know that's probably hard for you to understand since you're not a creative anymore, and you don't work in fashion."

Not a creative? The words hit Layla like a light slap. She wasn't totally oblivious to understanding the excitement that came from bringing inspiration to life.

She'd experienced it setting up her office, choosing furnishings to complement the custom mural she'd helped design.

And she was dropped into the deep end of creativity during her annual trips to California to see Kinsley, her best friend and roommate from college.

Kinsley opened a pop-up store every March selling prom dresses and evening gowns where she lived in San Jose.

For the past three years, she'd taken a week off in September to help Kinsley sew her creations in exchange for wine, decadent meals cooked by Kinsley's foodie husband and tons of much needed girls' chat.

And Kinsley's silence.

What happened in San Jose stayed in San Jose. Grandma Ruby, Tyler and Patrice might not understand that she wasn't shunning the family business by helping Kinsley.

Playing designer and seamstress for a week wasn't

the same as actually being one like Grandma Ruby. Or like her and Tyler's mother, Aisha, had been.

A vision of their mom in the past flashed into Layla's mind and a ping of sadness hit.

She'd been eight and Tyler had been only three when their mom had died from an allergic reaction to medication.

Grandma Ruby had stepped in to take care of them. She'd also developed their understanding of all things fashion related in anticipation of them taking over Sashay Chic one day.

But Tyler's creative abilities had captured everyone's attention, and Grandma Ruby had taken her firmly under her wing.

Layla's choice to become an accountant and not join the company had disappointed Grandma Ruby. But Tyler's phenomenal talent had filled the void.

Just recently, Grandma Ruby had praised Tyler's natural instincts for running the business. Why wasn't she supporting her now?

Tyler released a long exhale and laid her head on Layla's shoulder. "I guess I shouldn't have assumed my experience with a large fashion house would be appreciated. Now that I'm here, I can't just sit around and watch our company fade from existence."

"I know it's hard, but until we know more, there's nothing we can do but wait it out."

"Even though we know she's making a mistake? No. Someone has to talk sense into her."

As Tyler looked at her, Layla glimpsed the baby sister who would come to her with skinned knees to bandage, broken toys to put back together, and who'd cried on her shoulder as a teen after experiencing her first heartbreak.

Those things were easy to take care of, but this…
"I can't."

"You have to. I know you can fix this." As Tyler gripped Layla's hand, conviction and desperation showed on her face. "When it comes to business decisions, Grandma always values your opinion. She'll listen to you."

Chapter Two

"I'm not changing my mind." Ruby Morris pushed up from the wood table in her kitchen. "I have lemon pie for dessert. Do you want whipped cream to go with it?"

Thrown by the sudden change of topic from Tyler's debut to pie, Layla sat momentarily speechless in her chair. "Yes, but—"

"I'll make some." Grandma Ruby spoke calmly, but the look in her honey-brown eyes reinforced that, as far as she was concerned, the conversation about Tyler's fashion collection debut was over.

Ruby picked up the half-empty bowl with the salad she and Layla had just enjoyed with their late lunch of rice and jerk chicken.

Rays from the afternoon sun, shining through the

picture window overlooking the back lawn, brought out subtle golden highlights in her dark hair pinned in an updo.

Nearing her seventy-fifth birthday, she still had an eye for fashion. The crisp black pants and royal blue sweater she wore reflected the style she'd infused into the Sashay Chic brand. And so did the ebony wood cane with silver accents she planted firmly on the bone-colored tiles as she walked away.

While her grandmother stored the salad and found the dessert in the refrigerator, Layla gathered up their dishes and put them on the beige granite counter near the sink.

When she'd brought up the topic of Tyler, she'd been fully prepared for her grandma to lay out the facts for her decision. She hadn't expected to be shut down after asking one question: "Can we talk about Tyler's fashion collection?"

Avoidance had never been her grandmother's way of handling issues. And Layla had encountered something else she'd never sensed in her grandmother before. Unease.

Ruby put the pie on the opposite counter and took out a mixing bowl from the cabinet underneath. "Shoot. I forgot the heavy cream in the refrigerator. Would you get it for me?"

"Sure." Layla hesitated. Normally she would never push back on something Grandma Ruby said, but she couldn't just pretend nothing was wrong and eat lemon pie. Whatever was bothering her grandmother, they had to talk about it.

Taking a fortifying breath, she aimed for one of her grandma's soft spots—her love for her grandchildren. "Tyler thinks you're against her and that you don't want her to succeed at Sashay Chic."

"What?" Dismay flooded Ruby's face. "I only want the best for her."

"How is keeping Tyler from what she's always dreamed of, and preventing her from what you've always wanted her to do, the best for her? She feels blindsided by the decision about her fashion collection. If what she's proposing is too drastic, shouldn't you at least give her a chance to fix it?"

Ruby shook her head. "It's not that simple."

"Why?"

"Because you can't fix a jinx."

"A jinx?" Layla paused, not sure she'd heard her right. "You mean bad luck?"

"It's more than that." Indecision came and went from Ruby's face. "I have to show you something. I'll be right back."

She walked briskly out of the archway leading from the kitchen.

The nearby hall closet opened, and the sound of Ruby sliding clothes hangers aside and moving boxes echoed. Something banged to the floor.

Layla turned toward the archway. "Are you okay?"

"I'm fine… Stay where you are."

Needing to do more than just stand there listening to her grandma rummage through the closet, Layla rinsed the plates and silverware and loaded them into the dishwasher. What was this jinx stuff about, and what was her grandmother looking for?

Ruby returned carrying a thick photo album. She plunked it on the counter near the pie. "What I'm about to tell you, you can't repeat to anyone."

"I won't." Layla washed her hands and dried them with a paper towel.

Her grandmother flipped through the glossy pages and stopped halfway through the album. "The woman in the picture with me—she's the problem."

Ruby pointed to a photo of herself from decades ago wearing a black-and-white dress with a wide belt cinching her waist. She stood next to a blonde woman in a blue suit with padded shoulders. They were both laughing as they looked toward whoever held the camera. From their clothes and the volume and layers in their hair, it had been taken sometime in the eighties.

Layla took a closer look. "Who is she?"

"Charlotte Henry, my former business partner."

"When did you have a business partner?"

"It was a long time ago." A wistful expression came over her grandmother's face. "After your grandfather passed away, I was trying to raise your mother on my own in D.C., but even with two jobs, I was struggling financially. Becoming a widow in my thirties was something I'd never imagined happening. It was hard on your mother, too. She was only ten years old. Her grades suffered, and she started getting sick a lot.

"Someone I knew suggested moving to Bolan,

Maryland. It was cheaper to live there. I found a decent job with an office cleaning company, and I was able to rent a house with a nice backyard. It was a small, family-friendly town, but…" Ruby chuckled. "It took a minute to get used to everyone there, and two counties over, knowing everybody's business. Other than that, the change of scenery did us both a lot of good."

Layla tried to envision her mother and grandmother living in a place without mass transportation, major events or restaurants of every kind. Or her grandmother cleaning offices instead of running the apparel company she'd built to seven retail stores in Georgia. They had recently downsized to five at Tyler's urging, in favor of upgrading Sashay Chic's online retail site.

Holding back questions, she let her grandma continue.

"I met Charlotte working the night shift, and we became friends. I'd planned on doing some work as a seamstress on the side like I did in D.C., but I found out she was already doing it. Instead of competing against each other, we agreed to work together and capitalize on the areas we enjoyed. I had a hand for design, and she was a better seamstress.

"A year later, we had so much business, it grew beyond just a few hours a day. We decided to go after what we really wanted—our own dress shop. With a business loan and our own savings, we were able to buy a small storefront just outside of town that used to be a hardware store. It wasn't a fancy new building on Main Street, but the past owner had taken good care of the place, and it was ours. We were so excited. This photo was taken the day we opened Bee and Tee's Boutique."

Layla's thoughts went back to the opening of her business four years ago. Making the leap from the partner track at a large accounting firm to branching out on her own had felt like what she'd needed to do, but excitement hadn't been part of her experience.

Despite having Sashay Chic, and a few of her grandmother's and father's connections already on her client roster, she'd spent her first day in business battling nausea, afraid she'd made a huge mistake.

"Why the name Bee and Tee's?"

"Bee was my nickname and Tee was hers." Ruby lightly tapped the photo. "About a year after we opened the shop, some investors wanted to help us open another one in Baltimore. I was excited about it. But Charlotte couldn't see past Bolan. We argued. I told Charlotte her small-town thinking was like a boulder tied to our success, and I wouldn't let her keep me down. I would do it on my own. She said I was fooling myself if I believed I could manage a shop alone."

The way Grandma Ruby and Charlotte were smiling at each other in the photos on the page, it was hard to imagine the two women in an argument.

Determination filled Ruby's face. "I wanted to show her she was wrong, so I wrote up my own proposal for the investors. But they wouldn't meet with me. I was hurt and disappointed, but I also knew I was destined for more. I told Charlotte I wanted to dissolve our partnership and was leaving in a month. But things got so bad between us, we couldn't stand being in the same room together. All our time together, she'd been kind and caring. But after our disagreement, she was cold to me. It happened like a flip of a switch. I decided to leave right away instead of waiting. Charlotte's attitude said good riddance. I left with your mother and started over in Atlanta."

"Did you ever talk to Charlotte again?"

Ruby's gaze focused on Layla's face. "I saw her last week during a layover at the airport in Chicago. After so many years, I was willing to let the past go. But she wasn't. Charlotte accused me of stealing some spring design sketches from her. I told her she was remembering it wrong. Those sketches were mine. That's when she cursed me."

"She cussed you out in public? That's terrible."

"No. Charlotte didn't *cuss* me out. She jinxed me."

"What? You…" Layla stopped short of calling the idea of being whammied by a curse ridiculous. That might stop her grandmother from telling her the whole story. "What did she say to you?"

"That she'd wished since the day I left town that the design sketches would only bring me misery, and if they hadn't, karma was coming for me, and I deserved the worst. At first, I didn't think anything of it, but remember how my last fashion show before I retired was such a disaster?"

Remember it? Who could forget the event from seven years ago? A model had twisted her ankle so badly on the runway, she was carried out of the venue in tears. Then a ceiling tile had fallen on a photographer and broken his camera. Backstage hadn't fared any better. The lights had kept going out, making it difficult to get the models ready. To top the night off, the champagne fountain had collapsed at the after-party.

Yes, that show had experienced more than its share of difficulties but…

Puzzled, Layla asked, "How does what happened seven years ago fit with what Charlotte said to you at the airport?"

"I created the designs for my last show at Sashay Chic based on the spring sketches I'd brought from Bolan. Some of them were for clothes Charlotte and I had planned to feature in a small show highlighting one-of-a-kind designs, but I left before we finished organizing it. I hadn't looked at the sketches until seven years ago. I guess I was feeling nostalgic. I was proud of how far I'd come. And how I'd succeeded despite what Charlotte had said."

"You *should* be proud of your success. And since those designs were yours, you had every right to use them in your show."

"And nothing but bad came out of it." Resoluteness filled her grandmother's eyes. "I'm not trying to hurt Tyler. I'm just trying to protect her by not letting her pay homage to those designs. But I can't tell her or Patrice about the jinx—they'll think I'm losing it. And if I just forbid Tyler to use the Bolan designs for inspiration, she'll just keep questioning why and try to wear me down."

Ruby walked to the kitchen table and sat heavily in the chair. "I just have a bad feeling about it. I know Tyler's put her heart into her collection, but I could never forgive myself if her debut at Sashay Chic failed because of me."

Compassion rose in Layla for her grandmother. She could try to change her mind about a curse, but it didn't matter what she thought if her grandma believed the jinx was true. Honestly, what Grandma Ruby had described sounded like less of a jinx and more of a dispute over…*a measurable, tangible loss*.

An idea came to Layla. She went to the table, sat down and took her grandmother's hand. "What if I could get rid of the curse?"

Chapter Three

Four days after talking to Grandma Ruby, Layla drove her blue rental car up a slight incline. At the highest point, the sedan's headlights cut through the darkness and wisps of fog.

The tree-lined vacant road stretched for miles.

A shorter way? That's what the map app on her phone had claimed when she'd left the airport in Baltimore. Instead, she'd been driving for hours, and now the helpful guiding voice that had given her the darn directions in the first place had abandoned her and was no longer encouraging her to "proceed to the route."

But bad directions, and the hours-long flight delay that afternoon in Chicago, as well as having to postpone the start of her vacation from Thursday to

Friday, were worth it to settle her grandmother's debt with karma. Once that was done, she would head to South Carolina. In less than twenty-four hours, her biggest worries would consist of choosing which bathing suit to wear and whether she wanted a piña colada or a lemon drop cocktail at lunch.

As Layla drove through a curve, the fog grew denser, and she eased off the gas.

Another wonderful part of her vacation would be putting the gloomy weather behind her. She'd encountered cloudy skies since Chicago. Funny how she'd ended up stuck at the same airport where her grandma had last spoken with Charlotte Henry. If she'd believed in signs, which she didn't, she might have considered it a bad omen for the detour she was taking before her beach escape.

Visiting Charlotte in Bolan with a financial offer, on behalf of Grandma Ruby, was the perfect, advantageous, jinx-ending solution. Her grandmother would close the loop on the past. And Tyler would have the fashion collection debut she wanted. At least that's what their grandma had agreed would happen once the curse-breaking payoff was accepted.

But Grandma Ruby had also claimed, "From the look in her eyes, if Charlotte was on fire in the middle of the desert, that woman would rather burn than accept a thimbleful of water from me. Charlotte's pride always got in the way of her being reasonable."

That was harsh. But what was that corny thing her father always said about business disputes? No matter how angry someone was, making money always made sense. And from her experience working with her accounting clients, she agreed. Money was usually a reason for, or a solution to a problem. Charlotte would accept the offer, and the so-called jinx would be put to rest.

As Layla drove through another curve in the road, the windshield started to cloud over. She turned down the air conditioner, trying to match the weather outside the car, and grew warmer under her gray blouse and jeans.

Spring weather was so unpredictable. One minute there was rain, then the weather was cool, and the next—

Something leaped from the shadows.

Layla jammed her foot on the brake. Panic took hold of her as the tires squealed on the asphalt.

Veering toward the side of the road, the sedan bounced over uneven ground. Pitching downward, it came to an abrupt halt.

Flung back by the seat belt, Layla gripped the wheel paralyzed in shock. She stared at the trees only a few feet away illuminated by the car's headlights.

"I'm okay. I'm okay." As she whispered the words over and over, she laid her hand over her heart that was beating as if it had grown ten times larger in her chest.

She really was alright, and what was most likely a deer had made it safely across the road. And the car seemed okay, too. The engine was still running, but the front end was angled into a ditch.

Shaky from adrenaline, she dried her sweatslickened palms on her thighs and put the car in Reverse. As she pushed down on the gas, the car rolled back a fraction then stopped.

"No, don't do this…" She pressed harder on the accelerator, and the engine revved louder as the wheels spun in place.

Forcing her racing mind to slow down, she put the car in Park and turned it off. Her auto insurance offered twenty-four-hour roadside service.

Layla took her phone from the cup holder in the middle console. A quick search through her contacts brought up the number. She made the call, and…*no cell service.*

As she peered out the window, visions of everything from a hatchet-wielding stranger to large rabid animals to zombies slipping out of the eerie darkness crept into her mind.

Girl, this is not the time for that. She needed to keep her imagination in check and rely on common sense. The back road to nowhere led somewhere, and someone would eventually come along. She had to make sure they noticed her.

Tapping the flashlight on her phone, she glanced out the side windows. Water pooled under the driver's and front passenger side doors. But the rear doors opened above mostly mud, and they were closer to the road.

Reclining the seat as far as it would go, she climbed over it. One banged knee and a squashed boob later, she reached the back seat and her luggage. Rummaging through her carry-on, she dug out her socks and tennis shoes, changed out of her flats and slipped on a denim jacket.

Outside the car, she stepped into cold muck. Tamping down dismay over mud and possibly creepy-crawlies oozing into her favorite casual Jimmy Choo's, she held on to the car and climbed to solid ground.

Okay, this is good. I'm making progress. In the trunk, Layla found the emergency kit. She removed the handle from the car jack. *Out-of-control weirdos, animals or zombies beware...*

After setting up triangle reflectors, she ventured a few yards up and down the road holding up her phone, hoping for a signal...and got nothing.

Seriously? Could her luck get any worse? It was like she was—

No. This was not about the *j* word. This was simply a problem she had to fix.

Wait a minute... A few weeks ago, she'd been watching a movie about an apocalyptic future. The couple in the film had gotten stuck on a muddy road, and they'd wedged their clothing under the tires to get moving again. She wasn't desperate enough to give up anything in her suitcase for the cause, but the rental had carpet floor mats. Would those work?

Hurrying to the car, she retrieved the mats. Treading through water that was a little more than ankle deep, she stuffed them under the front tires with the jack handle.

The sound of an engine reverberated.

Layla scrambled up to the road. Raising her hand,

she partially shielded her eyes from the glare of a car's high beams.

Whoever was behind the wheel dimmed the headlights as they slowed and brought the dark truck to a stop.

The driver's door opened, and a man stepped out. His booted footfalls echoed as he walked toward her. The truck lights illuminated his wide shoulders, trim waist and long legs.

As he came closer, she could make out his jeans, dark T-shirt and part of his face. "Miss, do you need help?"

The concern in his deep voice alleviated some of her apprehension, and she relaxed her grip on the jack handle. "Yes. My car is stuck in the ditch. I just put the carpet mats under the front tires. I'm hoping that might get me out."

"That could work." He walked to the ditch, glanced down at her car then pointed behind him. "I've got a tow strap. Between my truck and the mats, we shouldn't have a problem pulling the car back on the road."

Relief flooded into her. Just like that, no questions asked, this guy was willing to help. And he didn't give off any weirdness that made her feel she might have to whack him with the jack handle to make an escape.

He steered his truck toward the opposite side of the road. After backing up a few feet away from the rental, he shut off the engine and got out carrying a flashlight. "My name is Bastian, by the way."

The combination of his flashlight and hers gave her a better look at him.

His dark hair was cut close on the sides and a little longer on top. A shadow of a beard partially covered his checks, angled jawline, and framed his mouth. Brown eyes with hints of green stared down at her.

He had a nice face. And better yet, she still wasn't feeling any killer, stalker vibes from him.

His expression grew slightly puzzled as if he was waiting for something.

Oh... She hadn't told him her name. "I'm Layla."

A small friendly smile curved up his mouth. "I'm sorry we're meeting like this, Layla."

The way his rich voice wrapped around her name, earnest and reassuring, eased her guard down a bit more. "I'm so glad you stopped. I thought I was stuck here for the night."

"Happy to help." Bastian opened a storage box inside the bed of the truck and removed a thick strap with metal hooks. "How did you end up in the ditch?"

"I swerved to miss something. It came out of nowhere."

"Probably a deer. You have to watch for them out here." He attached the strap to the back of the rental and the rear bumper of the truck. "Put your car in reverse. When you feel the tires rolling back, ease down on the accelerator, but let my truck do most of the work. We just need to take it slow and easy at first."

That sounded simple enough. "Got it."

As he hopped into his truck, Layla went to her rental, started the car then put it in gear.

The rumble of the truck's engine grew louder, and the sedan started rolling back. Controlling a leap of excitement, she did exactly as he'd said and pressed slowly on the gas.

Little by little, the tires broke free, and the car rolled back onto the road.

Yes! Layla stopped the car and turned it off. She practically ran to him as he got out of his truck.

A burst of happiness fueled her smile. "Thank you so much."

"You're welcome." Bastian's full-on grin made her heart flip in her chest. With that captivating smile on his face, he was ten steps closer to gorgeous.

His smile faded. "Damn. The storm is getting close."

"It is?" She followed his glance to the shadowy clouds obscuring the sky.

"According to the weather forecast, it's a bad one. Where are you headed?"

"I'm trying to get to a place called Bolan. But I think the app on my phone has the wrong directions."

"You're about ninety miles out."

"What?" If she'd taken the other way, she would have been there by now. Too bad the voice on her phone wasn't a real person. She would have filed a complaint and billed them for a new pair of Jimmy Choo's.

"We should get going." Bastian unhooked the vehicles and put the towing gear away.

She grabbed the reflective triangles. As she shone the light around, the carpet mats snagged her attention. The rental company would charge her for them if they weren't returned.

He came up beside her. "Is something wrong?"

"I have to get the mats."

As she moved toward the edge of the road, he lightly grasped her arm. "I'll do it."

Meeting his gaze, she didn't want to look away. He emanated reassurance and trust. It was almost too easy to lean on him for help.

Layla shook herself out of the trance. "You've done enough for me. I can grab them."

"My boots are sturdier than your shoes." Bastian stepped down and trudged toward the first mat. "Could you shine the light a little more to the left?"

She did as he asked then followed him with the light as he went to collect the second one.

His boots and the bottom of his jeans were caked with muck. Maybe he'd let her pay to have his clothes cleaned. It was the least she could do to thank him.

Crawling out of the narrow ravine, Bastian planted a booted foot on the asphalt. "Anything el—" The mud under his other foot gave way. "Shit!"

"Whoa!" On a reflex, Layla reached for him, but only managed to grab his shirt. Tumbling forward, she smacked into him.

As they fell back, Bastian cradled Layla's head to his chest as his other arm wrapped around her waist.

They hit the ground with a squishy splash.

Eyes closed, cheek pressed to his shirt, she recovered the breath she'd lost, inhaling the pleasing scents of laundry soap and woodsy cologne.

A groan rumbled from his chest. "Layla…are you okay?"

She opened her eyes. The rental car's headlights illuminated where they were in the ditch. "Yes. Are you?"

As she lifted her head, his hand moved away. His other arm went slack.

"Bastian…" Layla pushed slightly away from him. "Bastian."

He didn't move.

Oh no…

Chapter Four

Sebastian Raynes released a breath of relief. Layla was okay. But he'd fallen. How had that happened? Actually, he knew exactly how. Instead of focusing on making it back to solid ground, he'd been thinking about how cute she was. Under different circumstances, he would have naturally been drawn to her. He might have even asked her out.

"Bastian... Bastian?" Worry rose in Layla's voice as she tapped his cheek.

Ignoring the hit to his pride and how nice she felt on top of him, he opened his eyes. "I'm good."

Thunder shook the ground.

Holding on to her, he sat up as she awkwardly straddled him. "Can you stand?"

"I think so." With her hands on his chest, Layla

started to rise. Her feet slid from under her, and she dropped back on top of him. "Darn it."

As she wiggled around, their hips aligned, and awareness moved through him faster than the bolt of lightning flashing across the sky.

Get it together, Raynes. "Wait a sec." Grasping her by the waist, he dug his boot heels in the mud. "I'm more stable now. Try again."

Holding on to his shoulders, Layla pushed up. His hands naturally moved down to her hips as he gave her a small boost.

She found her way back to the asphalt, but he couldn't stop staring. The memory of skimming his palms from the dip of her waist to her enticing curves was like an indelible map imprinted on his mind.

The wind and rain smacking against his face snapped him out of it. Snagging the carpet mats that had landed beside him, he followed her.

By the time he got out, rain fell steadily to the ground. "Pop the trunk. I'll put the mats in."

She hurried to the car and opened the back of the rental.

As Bastian stowed the mats, he glanced behind him and up ahead. The deluge obscured the darkened road even more in both directions.

Hunched against the wind and rain, he went to the driver's side of the car, and Layla partially opened the window.

He leaned down so she could hear him. "The storm is heading in the same direction we are. There's a decent motel about ten miles up, the Woodway Inn. It might be best to spend the night there and get a fresh start in the morning."

A dubious expression crossed her face. "You said I'm only ninety miles out. And I already have a reservation at a place called Tillbridge. I think I can make it. I just need gas."

Bastian resisted the urge to object. Just because he'd helped her out of the ditch didn't mean she should take his word on anything else. "After the motel, there's a gas station. The intersection you want to take is forty miles after that. Turn right. From there, it's a straight shot to Bolan. But when you see the exit for the town keep going. A little farther down, you'll see a sign for Tillbridge Horse Stable and Guesthouse."

"Sounds easy enough." She glanced ahead then back at him. "Thanks again for helping me out."

"You're welcome. I'll be behind you until the motel."

He stepped back from the car, and Layla gave a quick wave as she drove off.

Bastian jogged to his truck and got in. A short time later, he caught up with her.

Pouring rain blew over the truck and gusts of wind pushed against it from the side.

Layla slowed down.

Just like him, she was probably battling the weather to keep her car on the road.

In the worsening conditions, her ninety-mile drive would become even more tedious. And with the amount of rain filling up the gullies on the side of the road, flash flooding was becoming a real possibility.

He should have exchanged numbers with Layla so he could check in on her as she drove. No. He should have tried harder to change her mind about trying to reach her destination tonight.

At the gas station, he would mention to her about the possibility of flooding. And if she still insisted on driving, he'd let her know that he was staying with her the whole way. It wasn't safe for her to be on the road alone.

Traveling with her would mean changing his route. He'd planned to spend a week in Alexandria first and then go to Bolan to visit family, but he could make a quick stop in town first. He didn't have to be in Virginia until Monday.

Bastian slipped the thermal mug out of the middle console, drank tepid coffee and grimaced at the bitter taste.

He'd get a fresh cup at the gas station to help him stay alert for the drive.

A few miles later, the lit sign for the Woodway Inn came into view.

Settling back in the leather seat, he accepted a shower, clean clothes and a bed weren't in his immediate future.

They reached the entrance to the parking lot of the modest-sized, two-floored, brick building, but instead of driving past, she made the turn.

As she stopped under the awning over the motel entrance, a breath of relief whooshed out of him.

Bastian parked his truck behind her car and met her at the glass door.

The bright lights gave him his first clear view of her.

Messy tendrils of hair escaped from her ponytail and framed her flawless sepia brown face. As she looked up at him, her eyes reflected curiosity and warmth. The heavy rain had washed away a lot of the mud she'd picked up in the ditch, but splatters of it remained on her tennis shoes and damp clothes, mapping out what she'd been through that night.

Undoubtedly, he looked the same or worse. "You decided to stop."

"I wanted to keep driving." Layla pushed the strap of her purse higher on her shoulder and glanced out at the rain. "But even with the high beams on, I could barely see the road."

Bastian opened the door and let her walk first into the neat-looking, burgundy-carpeted lobby. "I'm glad you did. I wasn't looking forward to following you." In answer to her arched brow, he raised his hands in defense. "I was going to be there just as a precaution in case you needed backup. The route you were taking tends to flood in weather like this. But first, I was going to try to convince you at the gas station to change your mind about not stopping."

"And how were you going to do that?"

"I hadn't figured that part out yet. Maybe invite you to have a cup of coffee and ask you to hear me out."

"Just coffee, no food?" A hint of teasing was in her smile.

"Would it have made a difference?"

"Pretzels might have worked. I had planned to buy a bag of them to munch on during the drive." Sincerity came into her eyes. "Honestly, I appreciate you wanting to make the effort to warn me again about the weather. You could have just waved goodbye and forgotten about me."

Forget about her? He wouldn't. A part of him would always wonder about the pretty woman he'd met on the side of the road. Where was she from? Why was she going to Bolan? Would he run into her again?

Keeping that confession to himself, he settled for telling her most of the truth. "I wouldn't have been able to sleep knowing you were headed into a hazardous situation."

At the front desk, a middle-aged dark-haired woman in a black-and-burgundy uniform came from the back office. "Hello. Welcome to the Woodway Inn. Do you have a reservation?"

"We don't." He glanced to Layla. "But we're hoping you have vacancies."

"We do." The woman with Denise on her name tag slipped a pair of glasses from the top of her head and put them on. "Let me guess. The storm brought you in?"

"Definitely." Layla took her wallet from her purse. "It's really bad out there."

"The weather has been terrible all week, but tonight is the absolute worst." Denise typed on the keyboard and glanced at the screen on her side of the reception desk. "It's a good thing you stopped. When it rains like this, it's a mistake to keep driving. Flash floods are common out here. One minute the roads are fine, then the next thing you know, your car has turned into the cruise ship *Wish I Could Change My Mind*. And that is not a vacation you want to take."

Bastian glanced at Layla. *Told you.*

As she looked at him, a small smile tugged up her mouth.

If he was reading her correctly, she was probably thinking something along the lines of, *Okay, so you were right. No need to rub it in.*

But being right wasn't the important thing. What mattered was that she was safe.

"You want two rooms?" Denise peered over her glasses.

"Yes, please." Layla put her credit card on the counter. "And I'm paying for both."

"You don't have to do that." Bastian dug his money clip with his cards and IDs from the front pocket of his jeans.

"It's the least I can do. I might still be stuck out there in a ditch if you hadn't come along and towed me out."

Denise smiled at him as if she were impressed. "What a gentleman. People like you are so hard to find these days."

"It was the right thing to do." He looked to Layla. "And that's why you don't owe me anything."

"I know. But I want to thank you. Please let me."

Her earnestness and a sudden desire to make her happy almost swayed him. He put his card on the counter. "I appreciate the offer, but I'm paying for my room."

"I'm sorry, but I can't take payment from either of you." Denise frowned at the screen. "We're sold out."

The vision of a hot shower popped like an over-inflated balloon in Layla's mind.

Bastian rubbed the back of his neck. "Are you sure you don't have anything? Just a minute ago you said you had vacancies."

"I know." Denise's expression grew apologetic. "But things have been a bit confusing lately because we're renovating. The last two rooms listed in the available inventory are actually still on the remodeling list. You see, they used to be part of one large suite, but management finally realized they were losing money on it, and…"

Talking with her hands, Denise tumbled through an explanation ramble.

Layla's heart went out to her. She also hated delivering bad news. As Denise paused, Layla took a much-needed breath along with her.

"This is such a mess." Denise pressed her hands to her cheeks and shook her head. "One of the owner's nephews, Alex, is doing the work. He finished painting and carpeting the rooms last week. All they need now is furniture. Anyway, I know that's not what you want to hear. But I feel terrible. This shouldn't have happened."

"It's not your fault." Bastian leaned in. "But I want to make sure I'm understanding correctly. The rooms are done. They're just not furnished?"

"Yes. That's it." Denise sighed. "Alex is so wishy-washy when it comes to keeping his priorities straight. He was supposed to put the furniture in the rooms this morning, but I heard he didn't come in because he was off-roading with his friends in the next county."

As Layla met Bastian's gaze, it was as if she could read his mind. "We don't mind sleeping on the floor. We'll take the rooms."

"Putting a guest in a room that isn't ready is against policy."

Bastian glanced over his shoulder. "Then we'll need to camp out in your lobby until the weather eases up. We're not driving into a potential flood."

Lightning flashed and thunder vibrated through the space.

Empathy came into Denise's eyes. "Under the circumstances, I'm sure management would want me to make an exception."

A half hour later, Layla rolled her small suitcase into the white-walled room and locked the door behind her. A faint smell of fresh paint and new carpet hung in the chilly temperature-controlled air.

Shivering in her wet clothes, she propped her bag against the wall, then gratefully slid the carry-on from her shoulder and dropped it beside her suitcase.

The clear plastic bag with bed linens, towels and basic bathroom amenities Denise had given her earlier sat on the rust-colored carpet near the floor lamp.

The storm had not only prevented her from reaching Bolan. It had also cost her a furnished room with a king-size bed at Tillbridge Horse Stable and Guesthouse.

A little while ago, when she'd called to cancel, they'd been so understanding about her situation. She wouldn't be charged for the missed reservation.

The door opened and clicked shut in the room beside hers, drawing her attention to the open connecting archway.

Aside from the furniture, the owner's nephew hadn't gotten around to installing the doors separating the rooms.

A knock sounded on the doorjamb. "Is it alright if I come over?" Bastian called out.

"Yes."

He walked through the archway carrying a white plastic tote bag with the hotel logo. "I was hungry. I thought you might be, too, so I went back to raid the vending machines in the lobby."

A hunger pang hit at the mention of food. Other than a snack on the plane, she hadn't eaten since her layover in Chicago. "What did you get?"

He opened the bag. "There wasn't much left in the machines. Cheese and crackers, a couple packages of M&M's, lots of expired jalapeño chips. I skipped the chips, but got the rest, and Denise gave me an apple."

A look of boyish accomplishment crossed his face as he held it up.

He looked so cute, she couldn't help but chuckle.

Bastian gave her a quizzical smile. "What's so funny?"

"I'm just imagining you scoring candy on Halloween as a kid."

"That was one of my favorite nights of the year, and I *was* known for my skill at finding the good stuff. And it looks like I've still got the magic touch." He put the apple back in the bag and pulled out a package.

"Pretzels." A wide smile took over her mouth as she accepted it.

"There's two more packages, and I also have bottled water, cups, tea bags and some coffee and cocoa pods. She gave us a one-cup coffee machine. We can set it up in your room. Here—take what you want." He offered her the bag.

She refused it and put the pretzels back inside. "We're splitting everything. And we should put the machine in your room. You deserve the bonus of having coffee first in the morning for helping me."

"I already got a bonus." He pointed behind him. "Take a look."

As he moved aside in the archway, she peeked into his room. It looked just like hers except for one very noticeable addition. A flat-screen television hung on the wall.

"Alex's wishy-washy priorities." They said it at the same time and laughed.

As Layla glanced up at Bastian's face, their chuckles dimmed to quiet smiles.

He shifted his stance, and faint static-electricity-like tingles moved over her arm near his chest. An invisible pull made her want to stay right where she was.

Was she the only one who felt it, or did he feel it, too?

His eyes grew more hazel green and for a second, she was lost in his gaze.

Bastian cleared his throat and glanced toward the flat-screen. "We could watch television over dinner—well, sort of dinner—if you want."

Did she want to share a sort of dinner with him? In the midst of contemplating an answer, the *"yes"* pinging loudly in her mind took charge. "Meet you in thirty minutes."

Bastian smiled. "See you then."

Chapter Five

Happy and relaxed from a long hot shower, Layla stood in the bathroom wrapped in a towel debating an important decision. Should she put on her favorite comfy green jumpsuit or a peach cropped sweatshirt with matching sweatpants?

"That shade of olive washes you out..."

Her sister's words playing through her mind narrowed the choice. Layla slipped on the sweats.

Before leaving Atlanta, she'd assured Tyler that she had a solution to her conflict with Grandma Ruby. But as promised to their grandmother, she hadn't told Tyler about the jinx.

Tyler hated being left in the dark, but she'd agreed to remain patient for a little while longer—something that wasn't her baby sister's strong suit.

Layla finished getting dressed. Skipping her usual hair routine, she blow-dried it straight, and put it up in a messy bun. As a last-minute touch, she swiped her lips with plum-colored gloss.

The sound of water running in the bathroom next door filtered in.

Thirty minutes was almost up. Was Bastian ready? Anticipation rippled through her. He was just next door but meeting him felt like…a date. Something she hadn't really been on since starting her business.

Not that she hadn't tried to get out there, but managing an online dating profile was like a crappy part-time job without benefits. And meeting someone in the places that were supposedly hot spots for singles wasn't working for her either.

Coffee shops—she was best friends with her Keurig. A nice bar—apparently, she was catnip for guys with the worst pickup lines on the planet, and who also couldn't take the hint when she wasn't interested in the least.

And as far as the grocery store, she had the items she needed delivered. Stuck on the side of the road covered in mud hadn't made the list. Maybe it should have.

After snagging one of the pillows from where she'd spread out the sheets and comforter on the floor, she knocked on the connecting doorjamb. "Hello."

"Hey. Are you ready?" Bastian came into view.

Whoa… No, she was not ready for the cleaned-up version of Bastian.

His slicked-back, damp hair cleared a path to his riveting eyes. She couldn't help but stare up at him. But lowering her gaze didn't help.

The navy T-shirt he wore molded slightly to his hard chest, and his biceps bulged underneath his short sleeves. His loose black athletic shorts hinted at muscular thighs that matched the rest of his long legs.

The familiar masculine scent wafting over the threshold took her back to earlier that night in the ditch, and how good it had felt to be that close to him.

Mentally shaking herself out of the memory, she focused on what he'd asked her. "Yes. Right. I'm starving. For dinner. Or is this almost dinner?" Nervous laughter escaped. She really needed to be quiet now.

"Yeah, almost dinner. That's a good way to describe it." He smiled. "I wanted to make it comfortable since we're watching television. But that's hard to do without a table or chairs."

Like her, he'd laid out the comforter and sheets for a place to sleep near his duffel bag close to the wall. But he'd also spread out a blanket a few feet away with the food, water and cups in the middle of it. Pillows were arranged on opposite ends of the blanket for them to lounge on.

The fact that he'd made the effort was enough and sweet of him to do. "It's perfect."

"Good." A pleased look reflected in his eyes. He pointed to the coffee machine on the counter near the sink. "I'm making hot chocolate. Would you like a cup?"

"I would."

"Have a seat."

She picked a side of the blanket and added her pillow to the pile.

He walked to the counter. "So what's in Bolan?"

"It took a minute to get used to everyone there, and two counties over, knowing everybody's business..."

Grandma Ruby's words flashed like a warning sign in Layla's mind.

Earlier, when he'd given her directions, she'd mentioned staying at Tillbridge, and he'd known she'd meant Tillbridge Stable and Guesthouse.

It was probably best not to mention why she was going there or who she was going to see. He might know Charlotte or someone close to her.

Layla went with a shade of the truth. "I'm just passing through. What about you? Where are you headed?"

"Virginia."

She'd almost rented a house near Virginia Beach instead of Crescent Beach in South Carolina. Where was he going? As much as she wanted to know the answer, she couldn't ask. Prying into his life while holding back details on hers wasn't fair.

Layla picked up the remote on the blanket. She turned on the flat-screen and found the channel guide. "What type of movies do you like?"

"Action, drama if it's done right. What about you?"

"I'm open to watching almost anything, but I tend to gravitate toward thrillers."

"Interesting choice." Bastian joined her at the blanket, holding two cups.

As he handed her one of them, she put the remote near the edge of the blanket.

He sat across from her. "Psychological thrillers or the flesh-eating-zombie kind?"

The sweet, chocolaty scent floating up from the cup tempted her into pausing for a sip. The taste of warm goodness didn't disappoint. "Psychological sometimes. Flesh-eating zombies—*only* if they're done right."

"Really? Which ones?"

"*Resident Evil* and *World War Z* are a couple of my favorites."

"I liked *Resident Evil,* too."

Not many people respected her brand of weird in the zombie movie department. Did he really know about the films or was he just making polite conversation?

"What's the last zombie movie you've watched?"

"Recently? I think it was *The Girl with All the Gifts.*"

"Really?" That movie had a slightly different take than most in the zombie genre. Maybe he did have an interest in the films. "What did you think of the ending?"

"What other option do you have when you're surrounded by a world full of nonvegetarians?"

"That's true." Laughing, she set her cup aside,

opened the bag of pretzels and dumped them out on a napkin between them. He did the same with the M&M's.

Over the next hour, their conversation moved from favorites to disappointments to recommendations.

As he told her about a zombie Western she hadn't seen, Layla stretched out and propped her head on her hand. After dumping in the second package of pretzels and another bag of M&M's, he stretched out, too.

Talking with him like this was so comfortable and nice. Who cared if he spoiled the plot for the movie? The way intensity and humor played on his face enticed her into wanting to hear him say more about anything.

The Walking Dead series came up, leading to a debate.

"No." He shook his head. "If season four tops season six, *Zombie Robot Soldier Beasts* isn't the best zombie movie ever."

She almost spit out a pretzel. "Zombie robot what? That's not a real movie. You made that up."

"No, it really is a movie…" As he told her about the film, Bastian leaned in.

The clean scent of shampoo drew her gaze to the top of his head. No longer damp, his dark hair had a slight bit of waviness she itched to run her fingers through.

"And then there's a group of scientists."

She'd heard this plot twist before. "Just scientists or mad scientists?"

"Actually, they're humanoid robot scientists…"

As he started to trace the plot on the blanket with his finger, she lost track of what he was saying.

Each stroke brought his hand closer to hers, and the silent wish that he'd touch her grew stronger.

Tamping down longing, she focused on his recap of the film. "Wait. Did you just say the robot scientists turn into zombies? What happened to the soldier-beasts?"

"That's the best part." As he reached for an M&M, his fingers grazed hers and a frisson of tingles ignited over her skin. "Elite soldiers blow up the lab, but they inhale the zombie dust in the air that has the DNA from the infected robots and it turns them into beasts."

Disbelief partially cut through her awareness of him. "What? Wait? Zombie dust? There is no way on earth that is even close to the best zombie movie ever."

"I thought it was a cinematic masterpiece."

His solemn expression almost made her apologize. Until she caught the gleam of humor in his eyes. "That is not a real movie." She tossed an M&M at him.

Bastian caught it next to his chest. "Google it." As he slipped the candy into his mouth, his amused, sexy smirk gave way.

His firm-looking lips looked perfect for delivering slow, long kisses. The kind with just the right amount of pressure that made you lean in for more and lasted until you had to breathe.

Imagining what her lips would feel like against his made her heart trip over a beat.

He pointed. "You have zombie dust on your face."

Pretzel crumbs...embarrassing. At least it wasn't drool. She brushed her hand over her cheek. "Is it gone?"

"Nope." He picked up a napkin. "May I?"

"Are you sure you want to risk it? Zombie dust could be dangerous."

He chuckled. "I'll take my chances."

The soft brush of the napkin raised goose bumps and her gaze to his.

Just inches apart, they stared at each other.

He was the ultimate trifecta. Gorgeous, funny, confident. No, make that a quadfecta. Just the possibility of earth-shattering kisses brought his mouth to the top spot on her list.

As a shaky breath escaped from her own, his gaze momentarily dropped to her lips.

Looking into his eyes, seconds ticked by. Layla lost count of them, held in the invisible, gravity-like pull, urging her to lean in with him.

They shared a lingering kiss. A long moment later, they eased away. As his gaze met hers again, she saw a desire that matched her own. Moving in at the same time, he tossed the napkin aside and cupped her cheek.

Their kisses alternated between slow, quick and light teases. Need uncoiled in Layla and the hunger for more grew inside of her.

Palm to his chest, she lightly balled the fabric in

her hand, wanting him closer. She yearned to press up against him.

Bastian moved his to her waist, keeping a small distance between them as he traced his tongue along the seam of her mouth.

The pleasurable sensation caused her to suck in a soft rush of air. He deepened the kiss, and she moaned, welcoming the increasing pressure of his lips. Their shared drift and glide as they explored each other through the passionate kiss confirmed her suspicions about the possibilities…and exceeded expectations.

As he slid his palm from her waist to her hip, she clasped his nape and rolled to her back. Partially on top of her, he rested his hand underneath her shirt on her belly. The heat of his palm seeping into her fed the need to feel more of his touch.

But Bastian slowly pulled away. Swallowing hard, he looked into her eyes. "I want you, Layla, but I need to know what *you* want. If you don't feel the same way I do, that's fine. We'll stop now."

Layla read past the longing in his eyes to the heart of the question. Did she want to sleep with him?

One night together. Fun without deep contemplation afterward. That's all it would be. It could also be a nice day-before-vacation kickoff. All of that was tempting…along with Bastian. He was sexy, and he made her feel sexy. He also made her feel safe.

Layla slid her hands up his chest. "Yes. I feel the same way. I want to be with you tonight."

Bastian's mouth covered hers. Between heated

kisses, they scooted over to the comforter. His lips sweeping down her throat made her heart beat faster. The inching up of her shirt and bra above her breasts shallowed her breath. His lips closing around one nipple and then the other, over and over again, made her arch up.

Layla gripped the back of his shirt and tugged upward. "Take this off."

"Not yet." The warmth from Bastian's mouth radiated over her breast as he caressed downward. Slipping past every barrier, he cupped her sex. "Let me take care of you first."

He glided into her then grazed his thumb over her sensitive nub. A master with his mouth and his hands, he delivered pure bliss, lifting her higher, taking her over the edge to orgasm.

As she floated in pleasure, Bastian stood and took off his shirt. Defined muscle rippling in his torso as he slid off his shorts and boxer briefs dropped her back to earth.

Every part of him was meant to be touched, explored…appreciated.

He found a condom in his duffel, put it on then came back to her.

Gaze holding hers, he nestled the tip of his erection at her opening, and she met his surge forward.

But he wasn't in a rush. His back muscles bunched and released under her fingertips as she met the rhythmic roll of his hips.

Maybe taking it slow was Bastian's specialty. If it was, she wasn't objecting.

She wrapped her legs higher on his waist, and delicious friction awakened places inside of Layla that made her moan in pleasure.

Hopefully, slow and easy was his plan for the rest of the night...

Hours later, the unfamiliar sheet brushing over her breasts, the thinly padded hard surface underneath her and the wonderful warmth shielding her back prompted Layla to open her eyes. Her mind filled in the blanks.

Storm. Woodway Inn. Bastian. They'd spent the night together.

Wrapped partially in the sheet and comforter and his one-armed embrace, she shifted her legs from being intertwined with his.

"Hey." Sleepiness tinged Bastian's husky tone. "You okay?"

"Yes." Layla spooned back against him, delightfully cocooned in his warmth. "But I should get up soon. I need to get to Bolan."

Once she was done there, she would drive back to Baltimore International in time to catch her evening flight to South Carolina.

"It's that time already?" He pressed a light kiss to the back of her shoulder. "I don't know what your plans are, but I'll be in Bolan in about a couple of weeks. Maybe we could meet up."

They couldn't. She would be long gone by then, but curiosity prompted her to ask, "Why will you be in Bolan?"

"To visit my grandmother." Bastian's voice grew softer. He was falling back to sleep. "She has a clothing shop—Buttons & Lace Boutique. You should check it out while you're there."

Buttons & Lace... Shock and his deep exhale raised goose bumps on her nape. She'd spent the night with Charlotte Henry's grandson?

As Bastian's breathing evened out, Layla slipped from his arms. The light she'd left on next door illuminated the way as she scooped up her clothes.

So much for fun and no deep contemplation. What were the chances of something like this happening? What was she going to say to him when he woke up?

Hey, funny story, our grandmothers used to be business partners back in the day, but now they can't stand each other. And oh, by the way, your grandmother put a jinx on my grandmother... That would go over well.

Tiptoeing to the other room, Layla paused and peeked over at him.

Bastian slept soundly on his back, the sheet riding low on his hips.

The last few hours had been the best she'd experienced with a guy in a long time. Strangely that included the two of them working together to get her rental car out of the ditch and finding shelter from the storm. And their in-depth conversation about zombie movies.

The only consequence she'd imagined from last night was remembering him with a smile on her face.

Why did she have to muddy that up with a potentially awkward conversation?

Or did she?

She wouldn't have to talk to him at all if she left before he woke up. Later on, if he did find out who she was, maybe he would choose to focus on how much they'd enjoyed each other, instead of what happened between their grandmothers in the past.

Layla got ready to leave, praying he wouldn't wake up. Less than an hour later, she walked through the connecting door and paused at the threshold of his room.

Bastian still slept. He looked so peaceful.

In her room, she found a pen and the flyer Denise had given her with the motel's checkout info. After jotting a quick note, she slipped off the candy-apple-red pumps she'd paired with navy slacks and a light blue blouse and crept into his room.

Retrieving the last package of pretzels from the blanket, she put them with the note near the coffee maker.

Moments later, outside of the motel room, she closed the door softly behind her and breathed a sigh of relief that she'd made her escape.

But as she wheeled her suitcase to the car, a reluctance to leave came over her. Layla kept walking.

She was making the right choice.

Chapter Six

WELCOME TO BOLAN. FRIENDS AND SMILES FOR MILES LIVE HERE.

A small bit of excitement leaped inside of Layla as she passed the sign. Just three miles to go until she reached downtown. And she'd made it in record time. It was just past nine thirty. According to Buttons & Lace's website, the store opened at nine.

Calling days earlier and speaking with Charlotte had crossed her mind, but so had Charlotte hanging up on her as soon as she mentioned Ruby's name. Face-to-face, she had a better chance of Charlotte hearing her out. But she had to get there first.

Layla pressed down on the accelerator. As she

passed an opening in the trees, she spotted a sheriff's car.

Seconds later, the car pulled onto the road behind her. The flashers on its roof lit up.

I'm over the speed limit. Crap.

In anticipation of the siren, Layla slowed down, preparing to pull over.

But the sheriff's car blew past.

She let out a pent-up breath. *Thank you.*

A few miles up ahead, presumably the same sheriff's car blocked her lane.

A deputy in a tan hat and uniform stood near the vehicle.

As Layla came closer, she obeyed his hand signal and stopped.

She opened the driver's side window. "Hello."

"Ma'am." The good-looking, bronze-skinned deputy gave a quick nod. "You're heading to Bolan?"

"Yes." From the expression on his face, she anticipated bad news.

"A pipe just burst and the main road into town is flooded. You'll have to take Colton Road." He glanced at her bags on the back seat. "Do you need directions?"

"Please."

"Make a U-turn. Two exits past the one for the interstate is the one for Colton Road. Exit, take the left. Keep following the signs to town." A polite smile tipped up his mouth as he pinned her with a direct stare. "And be sure to pay attention to the speed limit."

From the look in his eyes, she'd dodged a ticket. "I will. Thank you."

Layla followed his directions and got off on the Colton Road exit.

On the four-lane road, modern two-story houses and older-looking white clapboard homes sat back in the trees.

Acres of land separated the houses, and a few of them had barns with horses and cows grazing nearby or crops in a field.

She glimpsed a handwritten sign for classes on making herb-infused cooking oils, and farther up, a billboard advertised tours of a honeybee farm a few miles away.

She'd never done either of those things before. They might be fun with the right person…like Bastian.

She envisioned him laughing at the note she'd put with the pretzels. Had he left the motel yet?

Last night, she'd spotted a T-shirt in his bag with army insignia on it. And his haircut could pass for someone in the military as well. Was he stationed in Virginia?

If he was in the area, under different circumstances, she would have strongly considered a stopover flight in D.C. on her way back home to Atlanta. The fee to change her ticket would have been worth it to see him again.

Layla's mind traveled back to her night with Bastian. A flush of heat and longing swept over her, and she blew out a long breath. Before she spoke with

Charlotte, she really needed to put *that* image out of her mind.

Forcing thoughts of Bastian aside, she focused on the tranquil view and driving the speed limit.

Colton Road split into two and she veered right as the sign indicated.

Miles later, the countryside transformed into entrances to private subdivisions, and then a neighborhood with nearly identical houses and neat lawns.

Farther down, joggers ran an oval trail surrounding a park where a crowd cheered children playing soccer. More people supervised children at a playground.

"A small, family-friendly town..."

That's how Grandma Ruby had described Bolan decades ago. It appeared to be the same now.

Arriving at Main Street, she took a left. The central thoroughfare split into two, bordering an area with neatly cut grass and flowering bushes in the middle of town.

In the center square, old-fashioned-style streetlamps lined paths cutting through the grass. Sun glistened off the water cascading from a stone-fountain centerpiece. People sat on the park benches, reading, chatting and enjoying the view.

On the sidewalk, shoppers drifted into the connected businesses lining the street in strip mall fashion. The Bolan Book Attic, Flower Wonderland Florist Shop, an ice cream parlor. None of them was the place she was looking for.

Following the flow of traffic, she turned right and crossed to the other side of Main Street.

A two-story, light-colored brick building sat on the corner with Brewed Haven Café stenciled on the large storefront window. From the number of customers filing in and coming out with cardboard coffee cups, that was the local hot spot.

She'd check it out before leaving town.

A car vacated a parking spot along the sidewalk across from the café and she nabbed the space.

Next to where she'd parked, a sign with the names and street numbers of the shops provided helpful directional arrows.

Buttons & Lace Boutique was down the street.

As Layla wove through the few pedestrians on the sidewalk, she tucked her purse under her arm. She had a brief document for Charlotte to sign outlining a few simple terms for the payoff. Mainly that this was a one-time offer and a simple gesture of goodwill.

Two stores away, she took a deep breath, and put on her game face. Businesslike but personable. Open to both sides of the Bee and Tee's Boutique situation without assigning blame. Charlotte and Grandma Ruby had their own points of view on what happened back then, and she wasn't there to change Charlotte's mind. Did she have a problem with the woman wishing the worst on her grandmother? Definitely. But dwelling on that wouldn't solve the problem. She was advocating for peace and the closing of a difficult chapter in both of the women's lives.

Arriving at the boutique, she reached for the door and pulled.

It didn't open.

Layla peered through the window.

The lights were on.

A turned over stepladder and box lay on the floor near a shoe display along the wall.

Across the store, piles of clothes sat on the counter at the cashier station.

Someone had been there. Maybe Charlotte?

Layla glanced up and down the street, but she didn't spot anyone hurrying to open the place.

But there were lots of people carrying cups of coffee from Brewed Haven.

Layla headed toward the café. Noticing she was moving faster than everyone else, she slowed down.

Shedding the hurry-up-and-go mentality she embraced in the city would happen a lot easier sitting on the beach.

Hopefully by the time she fueled up on caffeine, and one of those jumbo cinnamon rolls she'd just spotted, and made a quick stop at the bookstore for a couple of beach reads, Charlotte would be at the store.

Where was she? No judgment, but the place was sort of a mess.

The slamming of doors, voices and a crying child brought Bastian fully awake.

A sliver of light peeked past the blackout curtains on the window. It was morning.

Rising to a sitting position, he took in the silence. He didn't have to get up and look around to know Layla was gone.

It was surprising she'd been able to leave without him realizing it. Just a few weeks out of the army, and his situational awareness had already gone to hell. Or had he just felt that comfortable around her? He hadn't been that relaxed or slept as soundly since...he couldn't remember.

As he got up and slipped on his shorts, his gaze drifted to where Layla had lain beside him. She'd left without saying goodbye.

Maybe that shouldn't have been a total surprise. Yesterday, when he'd asked her about Bolan, she'd changed the subject, and he'd taken the hint. She wasn't interested in sharing personal details. Last night was about no strings or expectations. He knew the drill.

As he walked toward the bathroom, a package of pretzels and a paper propped against the coffee maker caught his eye.

Bastian picked up the neatly written note.

Thank you for last night. Enjoy your coffee and the pretzels, complete with zombie dust.
Layla

Disappointment lifted as he envisioned a teasing smile lighting up her face. He couldn't stop a chuckle. If she were with him right then, he would have felt that smile on her lips as he kissed her.

But his time with Layla was over, and he needed

to focus on priorities. He had a job interview to get ready for in Alexandria.

The last job he'd interviewed for was at the Bolan Quick Stop and Shop, a convenience store just outside of town. He'd been almost twenty back then, not destined for college and unsure of what was next.

A year later, the one thing he did know was that he didn't want to keep working at the Stop and Shop. And he also didn't want his grandmother worrying about his future like she had before she'd taken him in to stay with her.

Growing up, he and his mom had lived in several places outside of Maryland. When times were tough or she decided to flake on being a parent, she'd dropped him off in Bolan with his grandmother, for a few months here and there.

His sophomore year of high school, he'd started living with his grandmother permanently, and his life became more stable. But as much as he'd appreciated her looking out for him, he'd itched to move away from Bolan. He just hadn't known how to make it happen or where to go.

As Bastian jumped in the shower, his thoughts went back to the morning that fate intervened. An army recruiter had stopped at the store for gas and coffee. The sergeant had embodied the things he'd wanted for himself—confidence, purpose and pride.

He'd asked the recruiter questions about joining the military and took him up on the invite of stopping by the recruiting station. That decision had transformed his life. And he wouldn't change having spent the past twelve years in the army for anything, but when his last reenlistment date appeared on the horizon, he'd felt it was time to get out. And once again, an opportunity had been there for him.

"The job is yours..."

That's what Aaron Mackenzie, a friend who had gotten out of the military a few years back, had told him when they'd run into each other two months ago at Hunter Army Airfield in Georgia. And he'd been grateful to hear it.

But as the co-owner of MaxPointe Protection, a security company based in Virginia, hiring him for the close-protection-specialist position wasn't strictly up to Aaron. The panel interview that coming Thursday, along with the informal gatherings three days prior—touring the company's training facility and going out to dinner with a few of the close-protection specialists—were the determining factors.

The activities during the days prior to the interview weren't a mandatory part of the process, but they were possibly the most important. They would help give everyone an idea of how he conducted himself and if he was a right fit for the team.

Bastian mulled over what was to come, and a hint of apprehension tightened his gut. But he was ready for MaxPointe. His résumé was good, and he'd researched the hell out of the company.

As he got out of the shower, his phone rang on the counter by the sink.

Wrapping a towel around his waist, Bastian glanced at the screen. It wasn't a number he recognized, but it could be someone from MaxPointe reaching out to him.

He answered, "Hello."

"Hi," a woman's voice greeted him. "Is this Sebastian Raynes?"

"Yes."

"My name is Philippa Gayle. I don't know if you remember me."

"I do. You live in my grandmother's guesthouse."

"Yes, or at least I used to—I moved out a month ago. I'm calling to double-check on something. Have you spoken to Charlotte?"

Concern raised prickles across his nape. "No, I haven't heard from her. What's going on?"

"Charlotte fell at the store this morning and was taken to the emergency room, but she wasn't admitted. She said she would call you."

He strode to his duffel bag and dug out clothes. "Where is she now?"

"She's at home. Asha—Dr. Kyle—she took over Lily Weston's practice about a year ago, cleared her to return home but suggested someone stay with her. Rina Tillbridge and I were going to take turns looking after Charlotte, but she nicely kicked us out."

"In other words, her independent streak kicked in."

Philippa chuckled wryly. "Exactly. Dr. Kyle phoned Charlotte's emergency contact, but she couldn't reach them. I found your number on my old lease agreement. I thought maybe you could convince Charlotte to let us help. We're not trying to butt in. We're just concerned about her."

"I appreciate you calling me, Philippa. And she'll have plenty of help." Bastian started getting dressed. "I'm on my way to the house."

Chapter Seven

Bastian turned into the long paved driveway.

Up ahead, nestled in the trees, sat the familiar white house with gray shutters. A smaller version of the house sat farther down the extended drive yards away.

The trace of disquiet he'd felt coming to the house as a kid settled over him. Arriving there with his mom, Diane, had always signaled that their life, in whichever city they'd just been staying in, had gone up in flames.

His mom losing her job because of some nebulous reason. Her quitting a job for an even more nebulous one. The cause was never her fault.

"I tried... I couldn't... I wanted to but..."

And the list of reasons for her not returning to

pick him back up at his grandmother's when she promised him was even longer. And he'd believed every one of them…until the day he found out she'd lied to him.

Bastian tamped down the remnants of remembered hurt and disappointment.

Being in Bolan always messed with his head. He hated the type of memories the town resurrected. Love for his grandmother was the only thing that brought him back to the small town.

After parking in front of the side-facing garage, he got out of the truck. As he walked the path to the front steps, the scents of wildflowers, freshly mowed grass and honeysuckle blew over him.

Searching through his keys, he found the one to the front door. As he stepped into the light cream tiled entryway, Bastian glanced left to the beige-carpeted stairs then right toward the hall.

"Gran," he called out. "It's me. Where are you?"

"I'm in the living room."

As he walked down the hallway, Bastian passed photos hanging on the light gray walls. Many of them were of him at various stages in his life.

Near the end, sunlight shining through the windows in the living room reflected off the glass of a gold framed picture. It was of him as a baby cradled in the arms of his sixteen-year-old mom with his grandmother standing behind them.

In the living room, Charlotte Henry sat on the end of the light brown reclining couch with her legs up. A pair of blue satin slippers were nearby on the navy-white-and-tan-patterned rug. The cheery yellow oversize shirt his seventy-year-old grandmother had paired with blue leggings was at odds with the signs of her discomfort.

An ice pack rested on her right knee, which was in a brace, and her right wrist, wrapped in a fitted splint, was propped up on a turquoise-and-beige throw pillow on the arm of the couch.

A worn-out expression with hints of pain diminished the ageless glow that usually shone on her face, but as she tucked her near-chin-length silvery-blond hair behind her ear, she beamed a huge smile. "Sebastian!"

"Hi, Gran."

"What are you doing here? Don't you have an interview in Virginia?"

"Not until later next week." He walked between the coffee table and an aqua side chair to reach her. As he leaned in, he glimpsed a faint bruise on her cheekbone. Unsure of her other injuries, he carefully embraced her. "A little birdie told me I should stop in to see you."

"I bet they did." She returned the hug with her good arm. "Which little birdie was it?"

"It doesn't matter." He laid his keys and phone near the gold-metal-based lamp on the side table next to her. "What matters is that you should have been the one to call me. What happened?"

"I was on a stepladder, hanging up some of the new inventory before the store opened. On the way down, I missed a step. It was a silly accident."

"A silly accident that sent you to the hospital in an ambulance."

"I could have driven myself and saved the money. Dr. Kyle and Mace made me go with the EMTs."

Bastian made a mental note, adding Mace Calderone, a friend from high school and a local sheriff's deputy, to the thank-you list along with Rina, Philippa and Dr. Kyle.

When he was deployed, the one thing that had given him peace of mind about his grandmother's welfare was that there were good people in town who cared about her.

He sat beside his grandmother and pointed to her wrist. "What did the doctors say about that and your knee? And that bruise on your cheek?"

"I have a hairline fracture in my wrist and I banged up my knee a little." She stated her injuries like a no-big-deal to-do list. Charlotte raised her hand toward her face. "And this looks worse than it is. I thought I covered it with makeup. I better put on more concealer before I go."

"Go where?"

"Back to the store for my deliveries. I'm expecting some wedding dresses. I have a VIP bridal session tomorrow morning with the mayor's daughter, Eden. I also have a delivery from the wine shop today. And flowers from the florist and hors d'oeuvre trays from Brewed Haven. But those aren't coming until tomorrow. That reminds me—I should check on which sample bouquets the florist is sending me."

Bastian bit back telling her what she wasn't going

to do. His gran was good at giving orders, but taking them was a whole other story.

Calling up patience, he lightly patted her uninjured hand. "I know you'd rather be there, but one of your sales associates can handle it. I'll drop by the store and make sure everything is good."

"There aren't any sales associates. It's just me. Lauren moved to California last month, and Nealy quit a few weeks ago. She couldn't balance work with her class load at the university. I've advertised the positions, but I haven't found anyone suitable to replace them."

It was probably more like none of the applicants had made it past her intense scrutiny. So she'd been handling the store on her own? No wonder she looked tired.

He rose from the couch. "Where's your phone? You still keep numbers for important customers in your contacts, don't you? We'll call Eden. I'm sure once you explain you're hurt, she'll understand you have to reschedule."

"Reschedule? I can't. Eden might understand but her mother, Poppy?" Charlotte pushed the button on the arm of the couch, and as the footrest came down, the ice pack plopped on the floor. "All she remembers is how I forgot to order the dress forty years ago for her sweet sixteen. The only reason it happened was because my so-called business partner back then left me high and dry. Never mind that, since then, I've made dresses for every major function Poppy has attended, including her own wedding. She still harps on that one time."

He knew the story about the business partner that had abandoned his grandmother, and vaguely remembered the one about Poppy and the birthday dress. But whatever happened forty years ago, or now, wasn't worth his grandmother risking her health.

As his grandmother went to push up from the chair, she winced in pain. "Oh…"

Bastian took hold of her arm and guided her back down. "I don't care what anyone thinks. I'm in charge of what happens now, and you're not going back to the store."

"But you don't understand. Months ago, Poppy wouldn't even consider Buttons & Lace as one of the places to buy Eden's wedding dress. They went elsewhere, and I've been dealing with everyone speculating why. But now things have changed. The shop they went to at first can't deliver on the dress. The wedding is only six weeks away, and now Eden's giving me a chance."

Charlotte sank heavily back on the couch. "If I don't win them over, everyone will keep talking about it. And I'm sure Poppy's sister-in-law, Anna, will be more than happy to make it front-page news in that tattle rag she calls a newspaper. I can see the headline in the *Bolan Town Talk* now. 'Buttons & Lace Is a Bust—Couldn't Supply the Dress for the Big Day'."

"I get it, Gran, and I don't want you to miss out

on an opportunity either. But if you don't give your-self time to heal, you'll be away from the shop a lot longer. I'm here. Let me do the work. Just give me a list of what you want done."

"It's not that simple. The dresses have to be steamed and everything arranged in the fitting room." She shook her head. "No, I can do it. I'll just go in earlier tomorrow morning and take care of it."

"You could, but what was that thing some really wise woman I know used to tell me? Just because you can doesn't mean you should."

"Don't get smart. You may be an adult, but you're still not old enough to throw my own words back at me." Despite her admonishing tone, humor came into her eyes. And so did weariness. "Maybe what you've suggested could work."

"It will. You taught me how to handle a steamer, and as far as arranging the fitting room, we can set up a video call. You tell me what goes where, and I'll make it happen."

"Okay." Sighing, she pushed the recline button. "I can see there's no use arguing with you."

Bastian picked up the ice pack and laid it on her swollen knee. He'd won this battle, but unless he solved the Poppy problem, his gran would drag her-self out the door tomorrow before sunrise.

Maybe he could convince her to go in *just* for the fitting at the appointed time, and not open the store. But he'd have to square away the deliveries and the dress setup today before he tackled that sub-ject with her.

Bastian made Charlotte more comfortable on the couch with additional pillows and a blanket. He pointed to the items he'd arranged on the side table next to her. "Water, pain reliever, phone, iPad, the television remote. Do you need anything else before I leave?"

"No, I'm fine." Charlotte waved him away. "Now go before you miss my deliveries."

He sneaked in a noisy kiss to her cheek, and she laughed, nudging him away.

Just before he reached the hallway, she called out. "Sebastian."

"Yeah?"

As he looked back at his grandmother, she smiled. "I'm glad you're here."

Chapter Eight

Bastian parked his truck in the alley behind Buttons & Lace Boutique. The drive had taken longer than anticipated. Instead of the main route, he'd had to take the detour to Colton Road and encountered traffic.

As he got out, a sheriff's car drove up and stopped. The driver's side door opened and Mace Calderone emerged.

Smiling, the dark-haired, bronze-skinned deputy walked over to Bastian. "When did you drag into town?"

"A couple of hours ago."

"It's good to see you." As they shook hands, Mace clapped Bastian on the shoulder. He glanced at the boutique and his expression sobered. "I heard

Philippa Gayle got in touch with you. How's Charlotte doing?"

"She's resting at the house. Thanks for making sure she went to the hospital."

"It was the right call. I'm just glad the situation wasn't worse than it was. The tourists who saw her fall said she almost tumbled the other direction, toward the window."

"Tourists?"

"Yeah, they couldn't get in because the store was locked. I was driving by, and they flagged me down. But Charlotte wasn't too thrilled to see me. She got up and started yelling about not breaking in. She didn't want to pay for a new door."

"Are you serious? She was more worried about the door than you helping her?"

"Yeah, and she was pretty adamant about it." Mace glanced at a car with a loud engine passing by at the end of the alley. "But she was probably stunned from the fall and not thinking straight. Since she was talking and moving around, there wasn't a need to break in. I called Rina at Brewed Haven. She has a key. Dr. Kyle happened to be grabbing coffee at the time, and she came, too."

Almost falling through a window. Tourists helping her. A lot more had occurred than his grandmother had mentioned.

Bastian took the key ring for the store from his pocket. "I just appreciate everyone looking out for her. And I'm glad I was close by."

"How long are you here?"

"For as long as it takes to make sure Gran is all right. I'm out of the army now."

"How does it feel?"

"Good." Prompted by Mace's long stare, Bastian added a little more honesty. "And different. I wore the uniform for twelve years straight, and I was deployed for most of them. As a Ranger, mission came first. As a civilian, the priorities are different."

Mace nodded. "I know where you're coming from. I felt the same way when I got out of the Marines. But once you find a new routine, things will fall into place. Any job prospects?"

"Yeah, I have an interview with MaxPointe Security in Virginia."

"MaxPointe's a good outfit. I'm sure the interview will go well. But if you want to explore another avenue, the department's hiring. If you're interested in knowing more about the job, call me."

A call came in on the two-way radio clipped to Mace's tactical belt. Cars were backed up on Colton Road.

"Speeding tourists and traffic jams. That's all that's been going on since the pipe burst on the main road today. With so many impatient drivers, it's been crazy. See what you're missing?" Mace chuckled. "You too could be living the life, brother."

Bastian laughed. "I don't know. That might be too much excitement for me."

Mace walked toward his cruiser. "When things settle down with Charlotte, let's grab a beer. Or better yet, you can come by the house for dinner with me and Zurie."

"Zurie? As in 'the girl you had a crush on in high school but she barely knew you existed' Zurie Tillbridge?"

Grinning, Mace paused before getting in the car. "Your memory of the situation is off, but yeah, that Zurie Tillbridge. We're living together now. Long story. I'll catch you up next time we talk."

"Sounds good."

As Mace drove off, Bastian exchanged a nod with him.

Mace was good people, and he appreciated him mentioning the job openings at the sheriff's department. But working in Bolan as a deputy wasn't in his future.

The close-protection-specialist position with MaxPointe was a better fit. Travel, the right amount of autonomy, and he would use skills he'd learned in the army. And based in Virginia, he would live close enough to keep tabs on Gran.

Bastian found the key for the store on the ring she'd given him. He needed to call Aaron and let him know what happened.

Staying in Bolan for the next few days to look after his grandma was a given. That would mean bowing out on the preinterview meet-and-greets. But he would find a way to make it to the actual interview on Thursday.

Afterward, he would come back to Bolan and continue monitoring Charlotte's recovery. Otherwise, she'd jump back into working at the store sooner than she should.

As Bastian unlocked the back door of Buttons & Lace, knocks from the front of the store echoed.

Walking straight down the hallway with tan walls and oak flooring, he passed the closed doors to the office and a storeroom on the right. The door to the kitchenette on the left was open.

Just outside the hallway, the register counter to the side had dresses piled on top of it.

In the main part of the store, racks of clothing against the side walls were interspersed with floor-length mirrors.

Folded T-shirts, sweaters and other tops were neatly stacked on displays in the center of the space.

Near the storefront windows, a stepladder lay half-open on its side on the floor. Next to it sat a turned over box with purses spilling out.

As he righted the stepladder, the vision of his grandmother tumbling off it made his gut tighten. What if she had fallen in the storeroom or her office instead of where the tourists had been able to see her? He shoved aside the thought.

A young brown-haired, college-aged guy wearing black clothing and a burgundy apron stood outside holding a medium-sized box.

Bastian unlocked and opened the door embossed with Buttons & Lace Boutique in gold script. "Hello."

"Hi." The guy with Todd and The Lush Vine printed on his name tag gave a quick, polite smile.

As he continued to talk, a woman walking across

town square toward the bookstore caught Bastian's attention. She looked like Layla. His heart kicked in a beat. Was it her?

The wineshop associate shifting from one foot to the other, blocking the view, made Bastian focus back on him. "Sorry. What did you say?"

Todd held up the box in his hands. "I have the three bottles of champagne Miss Henry ordered."

His grandmother was worried about the cost of an ambulance and a glass door, but she was buying champagne?

Bastian accepted the box. "Thanks."

Todd stood there as if waiting for something.

Realization dawned. "I need to sign for it and pay you."

"Yes, but I also need payment for the last invoice. Is Miss Henry here?"

"No. She's not, but I can take care of the invoice. How much is it?" His name was on the business account. He could write a check.

Todd told him the amount.

While the guy waited near the door, Bastian dropped off the box in the kitchenette.

In the office, which doubled as a workroom, he switched on the lights.

Two half-dressed female seamstress mannequins stood near the sewing machine in the nearby corner. Disorganized shelves with fabric and sewing supplies intermixed with office supplies lined the walls.

Bastian crossed to the opposite side of the room where paperwork sat piled on the wood desk. His grandma was usually more organized than this. A busy store and working shorthanded had definitely taken a toll.

He searched through the keys, looking for the one that opened the drawers, but couldn't find it.

The buzzer for the rear entrance rang.

That was probably the delivery for the dresses.

He went to the back door and opened it.

"Hello." The delivery guy rolled in a dolly stacked with boxes. "Where do you want these?"

Bastian pointed. "The office is fine."

The delivery guy dropped off the load. "I have more in the truck."

"Okay. I'll catch up with you in a sec. I have to handle another delivery."

On his way back up front, Bastian took out his credit card. He handed it to Todd. "Use this one."

Todd took a handheld reader from the front pocket of his apron and ran the card.

Bastian signed the screen, and Todd assured him a receipt would be sent to the email on file.

"That'll work. Thanks." As Todd walked out, Bastian strode to the back where the driver was waiting near the door. "Apologies for the holdup."

"No problem." The driver handed him a small digital tablet with a space to sign on the screen. "I'm just glad Miss Henry finally has someone to help her again. She didn't need to be here day and night. That's too much for one person."

"It is."

The more he heard about how his grandmother

was taking care of herself, the worse it got. Before he left, they were going to talk about her making some necessary changes. Starting with the hiring of staff.

Bastian gave the tablet back. "Have a good one."

"You, too."

The man left, and Bastian walked to the office.

The stacked boxes near the wall added more to the clutter of the space.

His phone in his back pocket chimed with a familiar ringtone. He answered using the video mode. "Hello, Gran. I was just about to call you."

From the angle of the camera, she sat upright instead of reclining on the couch. "Did the dresses arrive okay?"

"The boxes look good. No dings or tears."

"I don't care about the condition of the boxes."

"I know. I'm opening them now." As he hunted for something to cut open the cartons, questions about employee applications hovered on the tip of his tongue. Now wasn't the time to ask. He'd tackle that problem with her later.

Bastian finally unearthed a box cutter. He set his phone on a nearby shelf and got to work.

"Careful," she called out. "Sometimes things aren't packed correctly. You don't want to accidentally slice into one of the dresses."

"Don't worry. I'm taking my time." After opening the box, Bastian set the cutter aside. He removed the white vinyl garment bag out of a sea of foam peanuts and held it up by the hanger. "It looks good to me."

"It's what's inside that counts. Take the dress out so I can see it."

Bastian hung the bag with the dress on a nearby rack and took off the vinyl covering.

On-screen, Charlotte leaned forward. "Okay, that's the sheath dress. Open the other ones."

He unpacked the other four dresses. The last one was made of several layers of fabric and took up space on the rack.

"I need to see the skirt on that one."

He took the gown off the rack, backed up and held it in front of him. "Can you see it now?"

"Yes. That's the one with tulle and lace. You'll have to steam every layer individually."

A light tap on the open office door sounded behind him.

"Excuse me," a woman said.

He knew that voice. Bastian spun around.

As Layla took him in from head to toe, surprise came over her face. "Bastian?"

Unable to stop a grin, he stepped forward. "Hi—" His boot got tangled in the gown. "Damn."

"Be careful with that dress," Charlotte called out. "Who are you talking to?"

Layla peeked past his shoulder. "I can come back later if you're busy."

"No. Hold on a minute." He quickly hung up the dress and turned to Charlotte on-screen. "The dresses are good. I'll call you back in a minute."

He ended the call and turned to Layla. "Hey."

"Hi." Her surprise morphed to uncertainty as if she wasn't sure what to do or say.

He approached her. "I missed seeing you this morning."

"I didn't want to wake you."

"You should have. Seeing you before you left would have been worth losing sleep."

"I thought you needed it for the drive. What are you doing here?"

"Isn't it obvious? I'm preparing for the zombie apocalypse."

"And a wedding dress is just what you need. I can see the logic." Layla's laugh hit him in the middle of his chest.

It was good to hear it. For a second, he'd started to think she hadn't been glad they'd run into each other again.

She stepped closer. "Seriously, what are you doing here? I thought you were going to Virginia."

"I was, but…"

Women's voices traveled down the hallway, and realization dawned.

He'd forgotten to lock the front door.

Bastian muttered a curse under his breath. "I'll be right back."

Chapter Nine

Layla glanced from Bastian as he strode out of the office to the bridal gowns. What was he doing when she walked in, and why was he there instead of Charlotte?

As she contemplated the talk she needed to have with his grandmother, and Bastian being there to hear it, the spark of happiness she'd felt in seeing him again dimmed.

Or maybe it wasn't a bad thing that he was there. He could feel the same way she did about their grandmothers setting aside their differences. He might encourage Charlotte to accept the offer.

A conversation between Bastian and a woman drifted into the office.

"No, I'm not wrong," she said. "Charlotte told us we could try on the wedding dresses today."

"It's not a big deal," another woman interjected. "We can come back tomorrow when Charlotte's ready."

"Will she even be here tomorrow?" the first woman said. "I heard Charlotte had some sort of an accident here this morning. She must be seriously injured if she's left the store in your hands—no offense."

Charlotte had been in an accident? Concern grew in Layla. Was she okay?

Impatience slightly shadowed Bastian's tone. "Yes, Charlotte was hurt this morning. She's resting at the house so she'll be ready for your appointment tomorrow."

"Our appointment was today. She either got it wrong or she forgot. Did she even remember to order the dresses?" the snooty woman asked. "Or are we on the same road I went down with her when she failed to make my dress?"

"Mom, please…" The other woman sounded miserable.

"What? I'm not being unreasonable. Your wedding is just six weeks away. We've already dealt with one wedding dress disaster. We can't afford another one. We have to know what's going on now. If the dresses are here, we should just try them on. If Charlotte has inconvenienced us today by not following through on what she promised, we'll go elsewhere."

Bastian's phone rang on the shelf in the office.

Layla read the name on the screen. *Gran.* Was that short for Grandma?

"Will you excuse me a minute?" Bastian said. "My phone is ringing. I'll be right back."

"Make it quick," the mother said. "We don't have all day. And if it's Charlotte, tell her I'm not happy about this situation at all. In fact, just give me the phone. I'll tell her myself."

Moments later, Bastian stalked into the office. "I can't believe this woman..." he muttered in a low voice. He went to his phone on the shelf and declined the call.

Layla lowered her voice to match his. "Who's out there, and why is she being so nasty?"

"That's Poppy Ashford, the mayor's wife." He closed the office door. "She claims her daughter's VIP bridal session is today. My grandmother has it scheduled for tomorrow. I don't know who's right, but I'm pretty sure Poppy is going to make a big stink about it. Believe it or not, she's hung up on something that happened with my grandmother forty years ago."

"Forty years ago?" Was holding decades-old grudges a thing in this town?

"Yep. And it wasn't entirely my grandmother's fault. At the time she'd just gotten screwed over by her business partner. She was in a bind."

Screwed over? Irritation prickled over Layla. Clearly he'd heard a version of Ruby and Charlotte's story where Charlotte carried none of the blame. And that wasn't true.

But she hadn't come to Maryland to get into a

she-said–she-said debate about the issue. She was there to settle it.

Still, wrong appointment date or not, it was selfish of this Poppy woman to believe Charlotte should be at the store after suffering an injury.

Layla laid a hand on his arm. "I overheard you say your grandmother had some type of accident. I'm sorry to hear that. Is she alright?"

"She hurt herself when she fell off a stepladder this morning. With rest, she'll recover. I know Poppy wants to talk to her, but my grandmother doesn't need this type of stress right now."

"Maybe you should just give Poppy what she wants and let her daughter try on the dresses."

He shook his head. "It's a point of pride for my grandmother to make the right impression. She ordered champagne, samples of flowers and food for their session. Not to mention, letting Eden try on the dresses without catering to them as Poppy expected leaves too much room for interpretation of the situation from her point of view."

"But your grandmother's hurt. Is Poppy really that heartless not to take that into consideration?"

"From what my gran said, she's the type who would leave a one-star Yelp review and spread the bad news to as many people as she could persuade to listen. And she knows almost everyone around here."

Ouch. "What about her daughter? It sounded like she'd rather wait until your grandmother is here. Maybe she can talk her mother down?"

"Maybe. I don't know." Bastian released a harsh

breath and closed his eyes. When he opened them, he narrowed his gaze on her face.

"What?"

"I know this is a lot to ask, but would you be willing to help Eden with the dresses?"

"Me? Oh no."

As Layla waved him off, Bastian took hold of her hands. "I wouldn't even consider bringing you into this if it wasn't important. But a Hail Mary pass is better than no play at all. I'll pop the champagne. Who knows? Maybe Poppy will drink enough to loosen that stick up her ass. And if Eden finds a dress she likes, and she's happy, then problem solved."

"Bastian…"

The ask in his eyes held back her objection. But she was there to advocate for a peaceful payoff, not get tangled up in wedding dress issues.

The hopefulness on Bastian's face was replaced by a lopsided smile. He let go of her hands. "It's okay. You don't have to say anything. If I were you, I wouldn't want to get involved in this either. I'll be right back."

He walked out of the office.

Bastian's glum expression remained in Layla's mind. She understood how he felt. Bastian wanted the best for his grandmother just like she wanted the best for Grandma Ruby.

And there was something else to consider. Poppy bringing up her forty-year-old grudge about her dress had already resurrected bad memories about Grandma Ruby and Charlotte's partnership. If Poppy left dissatisfied, once Charlotte found out she was Ruby's granddaughter, she might refuse to talk to her. And Bastian might not want anything to do with her as well.

But all that aside, what about him pulling her car out of the ditch? He didn't have to stop and help her last night. And he'd been willing to follow her through a storm to make sure she was safe.

Not helping Bastian now was the equivalent of leaving him on the side of the road in the midst of a storm. The exact opposite of his generosity toward her.

Layla put her purse on the shelf and strode out of the office.

Reaching the end of the hallway, she stepped into the front of the store and out on what felt like a shaky limb. "Hello. I'm so sorry for being late."

Near the register counter Bastian turned to look at her. And so did the older blonde wearing neutral heels, tailored beige trousers and a loosely tucked white shirt, most likely Poppy.

The younger blonde in a casual but stylish pink-and-beige paisley dress was probably Eden.

As Layla joined them, she looked to Bastian. "Charlotte tried to reach me earlier, but I've been having problems with my cell service. I didn't get her message until a half hour ago. I got here as soon as I could."

Looking up at him, she couldn't tell if he was upset or pleased. Had she made a mistake?

He didn't smile, but the endorsement was in his eyes. "Thanks for coming on such short notice."

"Oh, it's not a problem. I'm happy to help." She flashed a smile at the younger blonde with long soft curls framing her face. "Hello, I'm Layla. Are you the bride-to-be?"

"Yes." A smile lit up her light gray eyes and the delicate features of her face. "I'm Eden, and this is my mother, Poppy."

"Poppy *Ashford*." Her mother glanced over Layla from head to toe. Her gaze paused on the red pumps and her brows rose a fraction with a look of appreciation. "When did you start working here?"

"Officially, today. But I've been fully briefed on your VIP bridal session. The dresses are *absolutely* beautiful. You're going to fall in love with them. Why don't you two go to the…" She looked around. Where were they trying on the dresses?

Bastian glanced toward a blue archway on the side wall. "The back fitting room."

"Yes, right, the back fitting room. I'll pull everything together as quickly as possible. Please be patient with me."

"Of course we'll be patient." Eden gave her an empathetic smile. "It's your first day, and you're getting thrown into this."

"Excuse me," Poppy interjected. "Exactly how much experience do you have assisting brides?"

"I used to work in the bridal department at an apparel store."

That wasn't a total lie. As soon as they were

old enough to have a paying job, she and Tyler had worked as sales associates in all departments at every Sashay Chic store. The flagship location in Atlanta had a substantial bridal section.

"And what about today's fitting?" Poppy added. "Charlotte assured us we wouldn't be trying on sample dresses, and that if Eden did find one that was suitable, her first fitting would be today."

"I can handle that as well."

"I think that answers all of our questions." Eden nudged her mother toward the archway. "We should let Layla get started. Thank you." She smiled at Layla.

"You're welcome." Layla smiled back.

Giving Layla a quizzical look, Bastian tipped his head toward the hallway, indicating she should follow him.

In the office, he closed the door behind them. "Are you sure you want to do this?"

"Yes."

"Earlier, you hesitated. What changed your mind?"

"You helped me when I needed it. It would have been wrong not to do the same."

He stood in front of her. "Like I said before, you don't owe me anything for that."

"You helping me isn't the only reason."

He arched a brow, waiting for her response.

The explanation about being there to offer his grandmother money was too lengthy to get into right then. And while getting past the present predicament with Poppy was a way to ensure a better outcome with making the payoff, there was another very legitimate motive.

"Because I like you."

"I like you, too." Bastian tugged her forward by the hand and lightly grasped her waist. "On second thought, I think you do owe me one thing."

"What?"

A slow smile curved up his mouth. "That kiss I missed out on this morning."

He brought her closer, and desire blocked out everything but how good it was to feel the press of his lips on hers.

A long moment later, they eased away from each other.

Breathless, she took in needed air.

Bastian released a slow exhale. "I guess we should figure out our game plan before Poppy loses patience."

Poppy...dresses... Eden. "Right." Layla slipped from his arms. She had an important problem to solve. "You mentioned flowers and food. Is it possible to get any of that now?"

"I'll see what I can do. Anything else?"

"Wrinkled dresses won't make a good impression. Is there a steamer?"

"A handheld one." On the way out, he pointed to it on a bottom shelf.

Long minutes later, she had steamed the sheath dress, and taken most of the major wrinkles out of a blush-colored gown with a mermaid-style skirt. Two similar dresses with long sleeves, fitted silk bodices and A-line skirts were already passable. But the one Bastian had been holding up when she'd first walked into the office would take at least another fifteen minutes.

"I understand." Bastian came back into the office talking on his phone. "We'll take whatever bouquets you can spare. Yes, I can pick them up. Thanks." He ended the call. "Brewed Haven is sending over a vegetable and a dessert tray, and the florist said she can loan us three of their silk bouquets—a round, a cascade and a crescent. Does that mean anything to you?"

"Yes, those are perfect. It's not a huge variety, but it will give Eden some idea about which style of bouquets look best with the gowns."

"How are we looking here?"

She pointed to the last gown. "Steaming that one will take more time, but I need to get things rolling."

"I'll do it. Anything else?"

"No, it's showtime. And the dress, just focus on getting most of the larger wrinkles out of the skirt. I don't want to keep Poppy and Eden waiting too long."

Layla took the sheath dress off of the rack. Holding the top of the padded hanger with one hand, she swept her other arm under the skirt.

Up front, she walked through the archway into the large, beige-carpeted fitting room.

A raised square platform sat in front of a three-way mirror in the middle of the far wall. The doors to two changing rooms sat open on each side.

Poppy sat back on the curved teal couch in a sitting area. As she tucked her phone into her purse on the glass coffee table, she stared at Layla with an air of skepticism.

Eden, perched on the couch next to her mom, stared at the gown. Her cheeks turned pink with an expression of excitement. Like most brides, she probably had high expectations for finding the right dress.

"You're not a creative anymore, and you don't work in fashion..."

Anxiety gripped Layla, and she clutched the hanger a bit tighter. Maybe Tyler had a point. She hadn't been a salesclerk in a really long time. What did she know about helping Eden find the perfect dress?

As her other palm under the dress started to sweat, Layla hurried toward the first changing room. She hung the gown on a hook to the right of the platform.

Eden joined her. Smiling softly, she lightly traced the intricate lace bodice. "This is so beautiful."

"That's not the dress for you," Poppy called out. "Your arms are too thin. I know you asked Charlotte to order a variety of dresses, but you should just stick to a style that's closest to the original dress you picked out."

Eden's smile faded and her hand dropped.

Actually, Eden's toned arms would work with almost any style. Layla held back her response to Poppy's observation. But she wouldn't let momzilla take this moment from her daughter.

She spoke softly to Eden. "It's hard to tell which dresses work and which ones don't when they're on a hanger. And why not try on all the dresses Charlotte brought in for you to see, since they're here?"

Eden smiled. "That's true."

Layla went back out to retrieve the two almost identical dresses.

Bastian came through the front door carrying a box with the bouquets. He set it on the register counter. "I think this is it. The food's already in the kitchen with the champagne."

His expression reminded her of when he'd stood in the archway between their motel rooms, holding the bag of food he'd scored for them.

If she would have known who he was back then, would she still have accepted his invite to watch television? Would she have spent the night with him?

Bastian lightly grasped her hand. "Hey, what's that look about? If you're having second thoughts, you can still back out."

She couldn't. This wasn't just about helping him. This was for Grandma Ruby and Tyler as well. "No, I'm not having second thoughts, just hoping I can pull this off."

"*We* can pull this off." He crouched to eye level. "Aside from steaming that last dress, what else can I do?"

He could not hate her later on when she told him the real reason why she came to Bolan. "Can you open the champagne?"

Bastian gave her hand a squeeze. "On it."

Finally, all of the dresses hung in the fitting room.

While Poppy drank champagne and sampled the vegetable tray, Layla helped Eden in the changing room.

Eden stepped into the sheath dress. "I really like the lacework on this one. My original dress was just silk."

"If you don't mind me asking, where did you buy the original dress and what happened to it?"

"I bought it from a wedding gown designer in Philadelphia. Unfortunately, their bridal salon caught fire last week, and all of their merchandise was lost."

"That's terrible." Layla zipped the gown. "I can't imagine the stress everyone involved is feeling, especially you and the rest of the brides. I'm sure it's heartbreaking to have lost the perfect dress."

"I *was* a little emotional at first, but, honestly, I hadn't found the perfect dress." Eden lowered her voice. "Glenn and his family live in Pennsylvania. Ten months ago, Mom and I went there to meet with my future mother-in-law, Iris, to talk about wedding plans, and she blindsided us with a trip to the bridal salon."

Wow. A demanding mother and a pushy mother-in-law. Poor Eden. "That sounds like an awkward situation."

"It was *sooo* uncomfortable. Things got really bad when my mom and Iris started sniping at each other over which dress I should choose. I randomly picked one just to get out of there. I thought about going back to the salon to find the dress I wanted, but Mom and Iris might have insisted on going with me. I didn't want to offend them or risk a repeat of what happened the first time."

"Oh, Eden…"

"I was okay with the dress, really." As Eden met Layla's gaze in the mirror, her smile said otherwise. "It was close enough to what I imagined, and I was only going to wear it once."

"But you shouldn't have to settle for close enough when it comes to your dress. In the future, when you look at your wedding photos, you deserve to see yourself wearing the one that made you happy, not *almost* happy."

"I know." Eden slipped on the white lace stiletto pumps she'd brought to the store with her. "But keeping Mom and Iris happy has become the bigger objective."

But it's your wedding day. Layla held back the objection. She was there to help Eden try on wedding dresses, not judge her relationship with her mom and future mother-in-law.

She gave Eden a reassuring smile. "Well, today's fitting is all about you enjoying some champagne, trying on every dress and choosing the *right* one for you."

Eden's mouth curved into a genuine smile. "I like the sound of that."

The sheath dress was set aside but not because of Eden's arms. She just didn't like the fit of the skirt. The blush-colored gown was pretty, but she really wanted to wear white.

Eden tried on the two identical gowns that were similar to the original one she'd chosen months ago under duress.

She wasn't overjoyed or even awestruck as she took in her reflection.

Poppy did a one-eighty on her decision, claiming she really didn't like the style either but hadn't wanted to argue over Iris's bad taste in front of the designer in Philadelphia.

As Eden stepped down from the podium, she glanced at Layla. "One more to go. The fifth one is the charm, right?" She smiled but doubt shadowed her face.

Optimism was fading as quickly as the bubbles floating in the glasses of champagne.

Layla helped Eden out of the fourth dress and into the classic ball gown.

In the main fitting room, as Layla met Eden's gaze in the three-way mirror, the bride-to-be didn't have to tell her what she was thinking.

Eden hadn't found *her* wedding dress.

Chapter Ten

Poppy set her empty flute on the coffee table. "Well, that definitely isn't the dress. Charlotte's recommendations were wrong."

Layla was shocked to see a hint of a gloating smile on the woman's face.

Poppy picked up her purse from the couch and stood. "Luckily for us, while you were in the changing room, I made a call. The boutique in Baltimore I suggested we go to in the first place can fit us in this afternoon."

Eden's shoulders drooped and weariness replaced the disappointment in her eyes. "Any chance they can do it another time? I'm really not in the mood to drive to Baltimore or try on more dresses today.

And aren't we supposed to meet with the wedding planners in an hour?"

"I cancelled that meeting already. They agree with me, your wedding gown is the priority." Poppy snagged a cookie from the dessert tray. "This shortbread is excellent. Have you tried them, Eden? You really should."

"I was going to have some after I tried on the dresses."

Poppy nibbled the cookie. "On second thought, don't try them. Stick to the vegetable tray," she called out as she left the fitting room. "The last thing we need is you bloated up from carbs."

Eden's shoulders sank with a long exhale. "I'd really hoped one of these selections would be the one. If I had my way, I would just take this one. It's so close to what I had in mind." Eden lifted her hair out of the way so Layla could get to the back buttons. "I'm so tired of planning this wedding. If I didn't think my mom would stroke out, I would convince Glenn we should elope."

Layla started unfastening the dress. "Short of convincing your mother to let you and Glenn elope, is there anything else I can do?"

Eden laughed. "Well, you could confess that you're really my fairy godmother in disguise and make the right wedding dress magically appear."

"If only I could. You said this one is close. What's missing?"

"Well, I like the shape of this skirt but it's a little too poufy. And I wish it had lace on it. Not necessarily the whole skirt. And up here." Eve wiggled her arm partway out of the short sleeve. "I would really like it to be more off the shoulder but with the long lace sleeves like the blush-colored dress. Do you know what I mean?"

Layla tried to envision what Eden was saying. "I think I do. Hold on a minute." She went to the cashier's station and searched the drawers for a pen or pencil and paper.

The front of the store was empty. Poppy was probably hunting down shortbread. And Bastian? Where was he?

Layla found a small clipboard in a cabinet underneath with outdated forms for a holiday prize drawing and golf pencils. Spotting pink flyers on top of the counter, she grabbed one. Just as she'd hoped, the back of it was blank.

She stuck the flyer on the clipboard and hurried back into the fitting room where Eden stood in front of the mirrors. "Okay, hold still a minute."

Layla drew a skirt on the back of the flyer, trying to incorporate what Eden had mentioned. Sometimes, Kinsley showed her sketches of the dresses she was thinking of making, and she would add in a detail or two as a suggestion. It had been a while since she'd sketched a design from scratch, but it was worth a try.

At least Eden would have something to show the bridal shop in Baltimore as a reference. They might have a dress in stock that was a close match.

"Is this what you're talking about?"

Eden peeked at the drawing. "Yes, but more flowy in the back."

"Like with a train?"

"Yes, but longer than what you have there."

"So chapel length." Layla added more to the skirt in the sketch and drew the bodice. "You mentioned off the shoulder with long sleeves…"

As she added a few more details, Eden gasped and pointed at the sketch. "That's it! That's my wedding dress." She squeezed Layla in a tight hug. "You're a genius."

"Who's a genius?" Poppy walked in. "And why aren't you out of that gown yet? We have to get going."

"No, we don't." Eden held up the bodice of the gown and squared her shoulders. "I found my dress."

"Oh no." Poppy waggled her finger. "You are not wearing that."

"No, I'm wearing this."

Eden slipped the clipboard from Layla's grasp, scooped up the skirt of the dress she wore and started down the steps of the podium.

Afraid Eden might trip over the yards of fabric, Layla scrambled after her, grabbing the train.

Eden stuck the clipboard in her mother's face. "This is my dress."

Confused, Poppy took it and stared at the drawing. "This isn't a dress. It's a sketch of one."

"Layla will find it." Eden shot Layla a hopeful look.

Layla hesitated. She wished she could give Eden what she wanted, but how? "I'll search through a few vendor listings. I'm sure one of them has a dress that's close to the sketch."

Poppy dropped the clipboard on the couch. "We don't have time to wait. Eden needs a dress now. And what if you can't find it?"

"Charlotte made Chloe Daniels's dress in a short amount of time." Eden kept looking to Layla. "If the dress can't be found, Charlotte will make it."

Panic hit Layla. *Wait!* She wouldn't be around after today, and she couldn't commit Charlotte to anything, especially since she was hurt.

Just as Layla went to speak, Poppy chimed in, "Eden, darling, I understand. This is all so overwhelming. But that's why I'm here. I know what's best."

"No, Mom, I'm done." As Eden cut off Poppy with a raised hand, Layla felt the level of shock she saw on Poppy's face. "Someday I'm going to look back at my wedding photos with Glenn, and I deserve to see myself in the dress that made *me* happy. The wedding gown search is over."

Eden snagged a cookie and took a bite. Wrestling with the skirt, she marched to the changing room.

As Layla followed holding the train, she could feel Poppy glaring at her back.

Behind closed doors in the changing cubicle, Eden took a shaky breath and pressed her hands to her flushed cheeks.

Laughing quietly, she whispered, "I can't believe I did that. She's upset. Isn't she?"

"Just a tad." A spot tingled on Layla's back where

one of Poppy's imaginary knives had probably landed. "But, Eden, she's right. The dress is just a sketch. Maybe if you take it to the boutique in Baltimore, they can find it."

"I don't want to go anywhere else for a wedding dress." Eden clasped Layla's hand. "You're the first person who's set aside what my mother or Iris insisted I had to wear and asked me what I wanted. You've also made me realize I not only want to wear the dress that makes me happy, but I also want to look back and see how the people and places in the town that I love played a part in my wedding. That includes Buttons & Lace and Charlotte, and you, too. You drew the dress of my dreams. I need your help to make it a reality."

For a brief second, Layla saw Tyler's face instead of Eden's, and her heart softened. "I'll try, but…"

"Thank you." Eden hugged Layla.

Layla hugged her back. She hadn't promised anything. Just that she'd try.

When Charlotte came back to work, she could probably contact the vendors Buttons & Lace normally did business with and see what they had that was close to the sketch. Or maybe Charlotte would decide to make the dress herself.

After helping Eden out of the gown, Layla carried it out of the changing room.

As she hung it on a wall hook, Poppy cornered her.

She spoke softly to Layla. "You obviously don't understand the magnitude of this wedding, because if you had, you wouldn't have stuck your nose into it."

Layla leaned on tolerance as she adjusted the dress securely on the hanger. "I understand perfectly. Eden wants a wedding dress that *she* loves."

Poppy snorted. "Her loving the dress isn't important. Eden looking every inch the wife of a future senator is. But now she isn't seeing the big picture because you've gotten her hopes up about a dress that doesn't even exist."

"The dress is out there."

"It better be. You have three days to give my daughter what she wants. If you can't, Charlotte is going to regret trusting her reputation to a stranger."

Minutes later, Layla said goodbye to Poppy and Eden. Poppy's ultimatum reverberated in her mind. *Crap.* She'd been so caught up in wanting to help Eden, she hadn't thought it all the way through. And she'd made things harder for Charlotte. And she hadn't talked to her about the money yet.

Smiling, Bastian joined Layla at the front of the store. "Eden looked happy. Which dress did she choose?"

"We really need to talk about that."

A loud growling sound came from Bastian.

He laid his hand over his stomach. "Do you mind if we talk over lunch?"

Chapter Eleven

Bastian walked with Layla into Brewed Haven Café.

The scent of fresh coffee mingled with the appealing smells of baking bread and savory food.

In front of them, the people who'd just picked up beverages or desserts from the baristas at the curved coffee station walked to the alcove on the left.

More customers, many of them peering at laptops or their phones, sat at the round tables arranged in the middle of the cozy space. All of the beige couches decorated with purple throw pillows and tucked under the three side windows were occupied.

The larger dining room on the right with light wood tables along with purple booths lining the street-facing window were also mostly filled. At close to three in the afternoon, the café was one of the most, if not the most popular place in town.

Bastian spotted an opening and pointed. "Is a booth okay? There's one free near the corner."

"Sure."

With his hand lightly on her back, they followed the instructions on the sign near the hostess stand and seated themselves.

As soon as they scooted into the booth, a young, lightly tanned, dark-haired woman, wearing a purple T-shirt with a steaming coffee cup emblazoned on it, dropped off glasses of water and plastic-covered menus.

"Hello. Welcome to Brewed Haven. My name is Jenn. I'll be right with you." After flashing a friendly smile, she hurried to a nearby table.

Layla briefly glanced at the menu and set it aside.

He perused the selections that ranged from sandwiches to meatloaf and mashed potatoes and other comfort food entrées. "What are you having?"

"Soup and a salad, I guess."

"Make sure you save room for dessert. The owner of this place is famous for her homemade pies."

"Oh…that sounds nice."

As Layla sipped water, she looked distracted. And she hadn't said much since they left the store. On the other hand, she'd just gone twelve rounds with Poppy Ashford.

"Bastian." A woman's voice reached him over the hum of conversation.

Rina Tillbridge approached their table. A yellow

band held back her long braids. Her flawless brown complexion was as radiant as her smile.

Although she was casually dressed in a yellow T-shirt, purple apron, jeans and tennis shoes, she carried herself like the boss.

"Rina." He stood. "I was just talking about you."

"Good things, I hope. Welcome home." She hugged him and he returned the brief embrace.

Home. It sounded strange to hear that. In the past, people would just ask him how long he was in town.

He sat down in the booth. "Layla, meet Rina Tillbridge."

"Hello." Layla smiled. "It's nice to meet you. Bastian was just telling me you're famous for your pies."

Rina nudged his shoulder. "He's been away for so long, I'm surprised he remembers the café sells pies. But the way Eden was raving about you earlier when she came in for coffee, you're the famous one. She said you're the dress whisperer."

"Dress whisperer? No." Layla adamantly shook her head. "All I did was try to help."

"From Eden's point of view, you did more than just help. You've saved her wedding day."

Bastian spotted discomfort in Layla's eyes.

But she had saved the day not only for Eden, but his grandmother, too. Why was Layla backing away from the compliment?

Sensing the need to run interference for Layla, Bastian shifted his attention to Rina. "I appreciate you sending those trays of food at the last minute. I hope it wasn't too much of a hassle. I know you're busy."

"Hassle? Not at all. After what Charlotte did for Chloe and Tristan's wedding, all you have to do is ask, and my family is there for her and you." Her smile dimmed to concern. "She really gave us all a scare this morning. How is she?"

"In pain, but she's fighting me on staying home. But you know how it is."

"Oh yes. Philippa and I got a strong taste of how stubborn she can be when she wants things her way. We were so relieved when we found out you were close by."

"Yeah, me, too." He glanced to Layla. If they hadn't spent the night together, he wouldn't have slept in, and he probably would have already been in Alexandria. In a way, she'd saved the day for him, too.

Rina continued, "Don't forget, we're still around. If we can do anything to help, just ask."

"Well, there is something I could use a hand with. Could you spread the word that Buttons & Lace is looking for store assistants? I don't know if Charlotte has gotten around to advertising the positions yet."

"Sure. And if you need someone in the meantime, I can ask Darby. I don't know if you remember her. She's my dining room supervisor. She usually helps out at Buttons & Lace on her days off during the winter holidays. She might be willing to work a few hours. And if I have to, I can adjust her schedule to make it easier for her."

Relief pushed a breath out of him. "That would be great. Having someone with experience filling in will help me convince my grandmother to take at least a couple of weeks off from working at the store. She needs time to recover."

Rina nodded. "That's important. At her age, broken bones can take longer to heal. Overdoing it won't help."

"Charlotte broke something?" Layla asked.

"Yes. Her wrist—she has a hairline fracture."

"Oh no." A troubled expression came over her face.

Just as he went to reassure her that his grandmother would get better, Jenn stopped at the table to take their orders.

Rina stepped aside. "I'll let you two enjoy lunch. It's on the house." As he started to object, she raised a hand. "Consider it a welcome-back gift." She smiled at Layla. "It was nice meeting you."

"Same here." Layla gave a small wave but worry etched even deeper on her face.

They placed their orders—chicken-fried steak for him and a bowl of turkey-and-corn chowder soup and a garden salad for her.

What? No pretzels with zombie dust? Yeah, it was corny, but that's what he would have said to her if silence wasn't sitting like a wall between them.

She hadn't been unhappy when she'd first shown up at Buttons & Lace. But Eden's VIP bridal session had changed her mood.

When Layla jumped in to help, he'd only been focused on the Hail Mary she'd given him. And how Poppy wouldn't get the chance to kick his gran when she was already down.

What he hadn't thought of was how dealing with Poppy and Eden might impact Layla.

"Layla, I'm sorry. I shouldn't have involved you in the situation with Eden. I tossed you into the deep end with Poppy, and you have every right to be upset with me."

"I'm not upset at you." Her gaze dropped from his. "But you might be with me."

Reaching into her purse beside her on the seat, she pulled out a folded paper. After unfolding it, she handed it to him. "Eden didn't pick any of the wedding gowns that your grandmother ordered. She chose that one."

The drawing featured a slender woman in an off-the-shoulder dress with lace sleeves and a long flowing skirt. "Is this something she saw somewhere?"

"No. I sketched it based on what Eden said she wanted and told her I would try to find it. I'm sorry. I was just supposed to help her try on the gowns. Not get her hopes up for one that doesn't exist. I went too far."

"You gave my grandmother a second chance." Bastian pointed to the sketch. "If you hadn't done this, Poppy and Eden would be in Baltimore, right now, buying a dress at another shop."

"But Poppy expects to see evidence of this dress in three days. If she doesn't, she'll put the blame on your grandmother and go after her reputation." Layla closed her eyes for a moment. "I had no intention of stirring up your grandmother's forty-year-old bad memories. I was trying to do the opposite."

"You haven't. I asked for your help, and you did what was right. You tried to look out for Eden and my grandmother. What happened in the past was because of another person's selfishness."

"By another person, you mean your grandmother's business partner?"

"Yes. From what my gran told me, her partner only cared about herself. You're nothing like her."

Layla opened her mouth as if to speak then pressed her lips shut. "I'll stay and find the dress."

"You don't have to."

"I need to make this right."

The determination in her eyes puzzled him. "You told me last night you were just passing through Bolan. Don't you have someplace to be?"

"I can stay." Layla fiddled with the spoon next to her glass. "I'm in between places in my life right now. I'm traveling and taking time to figure out what I want." She dropped her gaze.

But not before Bastian caught the hints of uncertainty in her eyes.

He could relate. When he'd put his papers in to get out of the army, even though he'd known it was the right thing to do, he'd felt uncertainty. And discomfort in not being able to admit that to anyone.

Her believing that she was leaving something undone with Eden's dress, in the midst of whatever she was dealing with, was probably adding to the stress.

"I understand." Bastian reached across the table and took her hand. "I just got out of the army a few weeks ago, and I'm in the process of figuring things out, too. So it's settled. Well, almost settled. I need to clear it with Gran, and break the news to her about Poppy's ultimatum."

After lunch, as they stood near her car, Bastian held open the driver's side door. "Are you good with the directions to Tillbridge?"

While picking over the meal she'd barely eaten, Layla had made a reservation at the guesthouse. "Yes."

"I'll call you later and let you know what my grandmother wants to do."

"Okay." Hints of the conflict he'd spotted in her eyes was now written on her face.

He tipped up Layla's chin with his finger. "Are you sure you want to stay and help?"

She gave a slight nod. "Yes."

"Then do me a favor and stop worrying. We'll figure it out."

Cupping her cheek, he pressed his lips to hers.

He tasted the light berry flavor of the gloss she'd put on her lips before they'd left the café.

Layla flattened her palm against his chest. For a second it felt as if she were nudging him back, but then she lightly grasped the front of his shirt, extending the kiss.

She stepped away first, got in the car and started the engine.

Bastian shut the door, and his gaze met hers through the window as she drove off.

He was glad she was staying, but he also had a mild sense of dread. A part of him felt that if she remained in town, the connection they'd shared since last night could be lost.

Chapter Twelve

Layla took a pair of black flats out of her luggage sitting on the padded bench at the foot of the bed. A nap on the queen-size mattress under high-thread-count sheets and a sumptuous cream comforter would have been heavenly.

Falling asleep to the sound of the ocean would have been even better. But that was on hold for at least three days, maybe less if she was lucky.

Changing her flight again and delaying her arrival to the beach house had been almost painful. But it hadn't been as difficult as hearing Bastian call Grandma Ruby selfish.

When he'd said it, she'd almost told him he was wrong and blurted out who she was. But standing up for her grandmother then wouldn't have solved anything.

From what she'd heard about his grandmother, under the present circumstances, Charlotte would probably feel "screwed over" by Ruby again because of her. That would have impacted her conversation with Charlotte about the payoff and not for the better.

And Bastian might have questioned why she'd gotten involved with Eden's VIP bridal session and created the sketch in the first place. And even though she hadn't known him that long, him doubting her would have hurt.

But even if she could avoid him doubting her intentions about Eden and the dress, she couldn't avoid his feelings changing about her. Once she revealed who she was, and why she was there, he would see her differently.

"Do me a favor and stop worrying. Everything will work out..."

But the new connection they shared most likely wouldn't survive the stretch from attraction to being on the opposite ends of a long-standing feud.

She really did like him, and she wouldn't have minded seeing him again after she left Bolan.

As Layla slipped on her shoes, the sadness of that no longer being a possibility weighed on her.

The road to closure on the past for Grandma Ruby had gotten longer and more complicated. But at least the first step was clear. She had to find Eden's wedding dress.

Her dinner reservation downstairs at Pasture Lane

Restaurant wasn't until seven fifteen. Celebrity chef Dominic Crawford was cooking tonight. At check-in, the desk clerk had mentioned it and been kind enough to book her a table.

She didn't have a list of Charlotte's preferred wholesale vendors yet, but a basic internet search might yield a few promising results.

If only she hadn't left her laptop at home, but her beach vacation plans had included unplugging from everything, even her phone whenever possible. She would have to use the computer in the business center.

Layla snagged her phone and key card from the dresser. On the way out, she picked up the sketch from the bed, now in a manila folder given to her by the desk clerk.

Downstairs, she got off the elevator and went right instead of walking straight into the lobby.

The dark-wood-floored space held the light scent of lemon and pine. Navy couches in a small seating area to the right had a modern feel. But a few country-living-inspired accents, along with the gold-framed paintings of horses running and grazing in rolling fields, added just the right amount of rural flair to the decor.

Reaching a beige-tiled corridor, she went left.

A group of people waited to walk through the glass double-doored entry of Pasture Lane Restaurant.

A little farther down, a shorter hallway on the same side led to the business center, a small meeting space and the fitness room.

The business center with four desktop stations and a middle island was empty.

Layla sat at one of the stations and opened the folder with the sketch next to the computer. The drawing had gotten a tad smudged, and the train on the dress needed adjusting. For accuracy, it should probably be a bit longer.

At the center island, she grabbed sheets of printer paper and a sharpened pencil.

As she sat back down at the station, she took a deep breath fueled by creative energy and a bit of anxiety. Was the drawing she'd made for Eden just a spur-of-the-moment fluke? Could she do it again?

Layla drew the sweeping lines of the skirt. No. It wasn't right. *Not poufy...* She erased it and drew it again. Satisfied, she added lace details, taking her time, not pressing down too hard on the pencil. *Thin lines...not thick ones.*

It would have been much easier to do this with a sketch pencil and pad.

With each stroke of the pencil, the drawing of the dress took shape.

A guest walking down the hall and into the fitness center broke her concentration.

Layla glanced at her phone. Had she really been sketching that long? Shoot. She still hadn't searched for a match of the gown online.

Turning her attention to the computer, she searched the internet for dresses similar to the drawing. Finding a couple of possibilities, she transferred the websites to her phone and bookmarked them.

The alarm she'd set for her dinner reservation chimed, and Layla packed up her things.

After skipping breakfast and not having an appetite during lunch, she was hungry and looking forward to a nice meal.

In the cream-walled, wood-floored foyer of the restaurant, a young blonde woman in a crisp navy button-down and black slacks stood behind the host podium.

She smiled at Layla. "Welcome to Pasture Lane Restaurant."

"Thank you. I have a seven-fifteen reservation for one—Layla Price."

"Let me see…" The woman scrolled down the screen of a computer tablet. "Yes. I have it. Please follow me."

Patrons sitting in the green padded chairs at the light wood tables chatted happily over their meals.

The hostess escorted Layla to a four-top corner table near the front of the dining room.

On the other side of a wall of glass, outside lights illuminated the narrow wood deck and the lush scenery.

Earlier that afternoon, when she'd first arrived at the guesthouse, the beauty of the landscape had prompted her to take a long breath. She'd smelled the scents of rich earth, freshly cut grass…and the distinct odor of manure.

Being out here definitely wasn't the same as staying near the ocean. But it wasn't entirely bad either, just different.

Layla put down her things and took a seat.

The hostess pointed to the gray embossed card in the middle of the place setting. "Your server will be here shortly to answer any questions about the special menu Chef Crawford and Chef Gayle have created tonight."

"Thank you."

As she perused the four offerings, her mouth started to water. Crispy chicken and waffles with brown-butter honey, bourbon short ribs served over Carolina Gold rice grits, spiced prawns with sprouted seed-and-grain salad, and a squash-and-basil pasta dish.

When the server arrived, Layla already knew what she wanted—the spiced prawns and a glass of pinot grigio.

A short time after she placed the order, her delectable, mouth-watering food journey began.

An arugula-and-parmesan salad to start awakened her taste buds. The spiced prawns were a near orgasmic experience, and each bite of the berry tartlet for dessert eased her to the perfect finish.

Happy and content after her meal, Layla sat back in her seat.

She had Patrice to thank for her appreciation of a really good meal. Growing up, her stepmother had always encouraged her and Tyler to experiment beyond chicken fingers at a restaurant.

Their father, Theo, had met Patrice at a food-and-wine event. Three years after he lost his wife, Patrice had taught him how to smile again.

As a business consultant, she'd also advised Grandma Ruby on how to navigate a future without Aisha being there to take over the helm of Sashay Chic. In time, it became obvious that Patrice not only had a place in Theo's life but also with the company.

Taking a sip of wine, Layla recalled her stepmother's positive influence on her life.

When Grandma Ruby had turned her full attention to Tyler's creative abilities, it had become clear to Layla she needed to get out of her sister's way. Unsure of what career to choose outside of fashion apparel, she had accepted Patrice's offer to set up shadowing opportunities for her with colleagues in other professions. The experience at a large accounting firm had stuck with her the most.

At first, she'd felt torn about walking away from fashion. But once she committed to becoming an accountant, she put her appreciation for dressmaking and her sketchbooks away.

Layla's gaze drifted to the manila folder on the table. She opened it. The new sketch on top was a copy of the one on the flyer, but it better represented the details Eden had mentioned. Maybe she hadn't lost her touch.

But Grandma Ruby would have made a cleaner sketch, and Tyler would have had a ton of fresh ideas for the design.

Luckily, the dress she would find for Eden would be much better than the drawing.

A small ripple of excitement moved through the patrons around her, prompting Layla to glance up.

Dominic Crawford had come out of the kitchen.

The tall, thirty-something, brown-skinned man dressed in a charcoal chef's jacket and black pants walked into the dining room with a pretty Black woman around Layla's age. She was similarly dressed to Dominic in a tailored lime-green chef's jacket and a matching band securing her dark locs.

The two split up, greeting patrons on opposite sides of the room.

Chef Gayle reached Layla's table and gave her a friendly smile. "Hello, I'm Philippa Gayle. How was your meal tonight?"

"It's a pleasure to meet you. The prawns were excellent. Honestly, I wish I could have tried everything on the menu."

"I'm so glad you enjoyed it." Chef Gayle's gaze drifted to the sketch and her expression grew quizzical. "Would you happen to be the designer working on Eden Ashford's dress?"

Wow. Everyone in town really did know everybody else's business. But at least Chef Gayle hadn't called her the dress whisperer.

"Actually, I'm not a designer." Layla smiled. "I'm just trying to make sure Eden has the dress she wants for her big day."

"Well, Eden said you nailed it. When I chatted with her today about food for the wedding reception, she was so excited that the search was over."

"Oh…" The search wasn't over quite yet.

Chef Gayle glanced to the other side of the room. Dominic was almost halfway down the restaurant.

"I'll let you enjoy your wine. If you are interested in trying the other entrées, you should come to the Starlight Tasting we're having here at Tillbridge. It's the kickoff to a local promotion featuring establishments in the area. Dominic and I will be sponsoring a booth."

"Thank you for telling me." The event sounded like the one mentioned on the tent card in the guest room.

"You're welcome. And thanks again for joining us tonight." Chef Gayle moved on to greet patrons at another table.

Back in her room, Layla glanced at the promo card on the bedside table. Just like she'd thought, it was advertising the event Chef Gayle had mentioned. Something like this would have been fun to attend with Bastian…if the circumstances were different.

Layla's phone chimed with a familiar ringtone. *Tyler.*

She'd told her that everything would be worked out by today. But it wasn't.

Layla let the call go to voice mail.

Just be patient a little longer.

Chapter Thirteen

Bastian entered his grandmother's house and shut the door.

As he listened to the sounds of the house, he tracked her to the kitchen.

After lunch, he'd gone back to the store to clean up, but several things needing attention had caught his eye. The leaky faucet in the kitchen, a light out in the bathroom, loose shelves in the office, an accumulation of debris around the garbage cans in the alley, and several other issues.

He'd tackled some of the tasks and stayed longer than he'd intended.

In the kitchen, Charlotte stood at the sink, favoring her hurt leg. She was filling the electric kettle with water.

"I'll make your tea." He nudged her aside and slipped the kettle from her grasp.

"Am I allowed to do anything in my own house?"

He kissed her on the cheek. "You are. But why not let me wait on you?"

"I'm too old to wait on anything, including you." She lightly poked his arm before hobbling to the side nook to take a seat at the square kitchen table. "Time is passing by so quickly. Some days, I'm almost afraid to blink. When I do, it seems like an entire week has gone on without me. I guess the bright side is I'm still here to blink."

"Don't say that." Bastian set the kettle on the base to heat up.

"Don't say what? That I'm getting older and someday I won't be here? It's true."

Since he'd seen her last, his gran had a few more lines around her eyes. And the fall had slowed her down. But she was still driven as she'd always been, maybe a bit too much.

Someday, his grandmother wouldn't be there, but that wouldn't happen for a long time. He'd do everything he could to make sure of that.

He'd run into Dr. Kyle while he'd been in town.

One of the things she'd been concerned about was his grandmother overdoing it and not getting enough rest. He'd told the doctor he would make sure she slowed down and started taking better care of herself.

He'd already called Aaron to let him know what happened, and to tell him he wouldn't make the company tour and the meet-and-greets. But Aaron had felt it was best to reschedule everything. The next-best date for Aaron and his partner was in three weeks.

By then, Charlotte would be more rested and well on the path to healing. And at least one, possibly two, permanent sales associates would be on staff at the store. He would make sure of that, too.

Charlotte slid one of the other three chairs closer and propped up her leg on it. "Since you didn't call me back or answer my texts, I'm assuming all the deliveries came in and you took care of the dresses?"

"I did." Bastian removed a mug from an upper cabinet. On the drive to the house, he'd contemplated how to break the news and concluded there was no easy way through it. "Poppy and Eden came by the store this afternoon. They thought their VIP bridal session was today."

"They what? No, it's tomorrow. I put it on my calendar. How did they get the dates mixed up? Let me guess? I'm to blame for their mistake. And I bet Poppy was burned up about coming back tomorrow."

"About that, something happened."

"Is it so bad you should spike my tea with whiskey?"

"No. Plain tea is good." He opened the wooden tea box on the beige granite counter and took out a packet of chamomile. "And even if what happened wasn't good, you shouldn't drink whiskey with your pain meds."

"Says you," she muttered. "What happened?"

The kettle beeped and he prepared the tea. "Poppy

wanted Eden to try on the dresses today. When I tried to discourage her, she threatened to go elsewhere, but then Layla jumped in to help."

Charlotte ignored the mug and honey container he set on the table. "Layla? Who's that?"

"We met last night. I helped pull her car out of a ditch. She mentioned she was coming to Bolan. I told her you owned Buttons & Lace. She happened to stop by the store when Poppy showed up. When she overheard the conversation, she offered to help Eden try on the dresses."

Charlotte sat up straighter in the chair. "You let a complete stranger help my best customers?"

"She's not a stranger. And she has experience with bridal fittings."

A skeptical look crossed his grandmother's face. "But you said you just met her. Exactly how well do you know this woman?"

His grandmother wasn't prudish. She knew he had a sex life, but he wasn't getting into that topic with her.

"The point is, she helped Eden choose a wedding dress."

"Which one?"

Maybe he should have spiked her tea before getting to this part.

Bastian took out his phone, pulled up a photo of the sketch and showed it to her. "This one."

"That's not one of the wedding dresses that came in. That's a sketch of an entirely different gown. Did Poppy and Eden bring this in?"

"No. Layla drew it based on what Eden said she wanted."

"And now what? I'm supposed to find it?" Charlotte's cheeks grew flushed. "The wedding is in six weeks. That's not a lot of time to hunt for something this specific."

They had less than a week, but now probably wasn't a good time to mention that.

"Layla knows getting the dress is time sensitive. If you provide her with a list of the wholesalers you normally deal with, she'll search their available stock for dresses similar to the sketch. If she doesn't find anything, she'll branch out to other places. Once she has a few possibilities, you can run them by Eden for her approval and order what she wants."

Charlotte huffed a sarcastic chuckle. "A Good Samaritan *and* a miracle worker? Lucky me. Before Layla does anything, I need to talk to her."

Bastian turned off the kettle. That went better than he expected. He'd anticipated having to convince her to meet Layla. "I'll arrange for her to come by here tomorrow."

"Tell me one thing. Do you trust her?"

Layla hadn't done anything for him not to trust her. And he didn't make a habit of spending the night with people he sensed might stab him in the back, literally or figuratively.

As he leaned back against the counter, he crossed his arms over his chest. "I have faith in her actions. I believe she genuinely wants to help, and she'll follow through on finding the dress."

As she stirred honey into her tea, a pensive look shadowed Charlotte's face. "Tell Layla to come by here tomorrow morning at eight."

"I'll see if she's free then. But, Gran, do me a favor. Don't interrogate her."

"I have to ask her questions about the sketch or what Eden said about it."

"I'm not talking about the sketch or her conversation with Eden. I'm talking about asking her personal questions. When Layla and I had lunch today, she mentioned that she's taking time off to figure some things out. I get the sense that whatever she's handling isn't easy. I've been there. The last thing she needs is someone prying at her."

"I'm not the type to pry and you know that." Charlotte sipped her tea. "Next topic. I have a chicken potpie from Pasture Lane Restaurant in the freezer. Is that good enough for dinner?"

"That's fine, but I'll take care of it." Bastian nudged her out into the living room.

"Putting food in the oven isn't difficult. I can do it."

"What you can do is put your feet up. I saw Dr. Kyle this afternoon. She's concerned about you taking time to heal from your injuries, and I told her that I would make sure you did. She also mentioned that at the hospital, you listed me as your emergency contact. But in her office files, Mom is listed. She was wondering if you wanted to make some changes."

"I probably should. I filled out that paperwork

a long time ago when you were deployed. Listing Diane made more sense."

"Has Mom called you lately?"

"Lately, no."

He hadn't spoken to his mother in a couple months either. "I'm back now. You can just list my contact information instead of hers."

When Dr. Kyle's office had called his mother, and she didn't answer, they couldn't leave a message because her voice mailbox was full.

Unreachable was now part of his mother's MO, along with the patented excuses she'd added over the years.

"I'd planned to... I didn't know."

After putting the potpie in the oven, Bastian walked toward the back door in a hallway off the kitchen. "I'm going to the guest cottage for a few minutes. I'll be back before the food is done. Text me if you need anything."

"Okay."

Outside, he found the flashlight in his truck. He used it to light the way down an extension of the gravel driveway, leading to the smaller house. It looked almost the same as his gran's place, but it had a single-door, front-facing garage and a porch surrounded by a white railing.

If Layla hadn't been able to get a room at the Tillbridge guesthouse, he would have offered Charlotte's guest cottage as a place to stay.

He should probably call her about meeting tomorrow before it got too late.

Bastian slipped his phone from his back pocket and called Layla. They'd traded numbers before leaving Brewed Haven.

Her phone rang and went to voice mail.

Rather than leave a message, he sent a text.

Can you drop by my grandmother's house tomorrow morning at eight?

He tapped in the address.

Layla didn't respond.

Bastian tucked his phone back into his pocket and inspected the cottage for any necessary repairs.

The two-bedroom house with a bathroom, living room and a kitchen looked in good shape. But while he was around, he would give the inside a fresh coat of paint and clean up the yard.

Bastian briefly checked outside the house. Nothing noticeable popped out at him. He would look around more thoroughly in the morning.

But what was standing out in his mind was that Layla still hadn't responded.

She'd driven to Tillbridge hours ago. Maybe he should call the guesthouse and make sure she arrived.

But she could have changed her mind about helping find the dress and left town instead.

"Do you trust her?"

He'd told his grandmother that Layla would follow through on finding the dress. But she didn't owe him or his grandmother anything. Just because they'd spent the night together and were attracted to each other, didn't bind them together as a couple.

Maybe he'd misjudged her. Acceptance took some of the edge off of disappointment. She was looking for something in her life, and hopefully, wherever she ended up, she'd find it.

His phone chimed.

Bastian glanced at the text. It was from Layla. A pent-up breath eased out of him as he read her response.

I'll be there.

Chapter Fourteen

Layla turned into the wide, extended driveway leading to Charlotte's house.

As she drove in, a blue car passed her on the way out.

She parked in front of the side-facing garage. Grabbing her purse from the passenger seat along with the manila folder, she got out of her rental.

Walking down the pathway to the porch, she brushed a speck of lint from the arm of her tan sweater. She hadn't packed business clothing. Hopefully the red-and-beige dress with spaghetti straps under it, and her trusty red pumps, were professional-looking enough for the meeting.

The front door opened, and Bastian came out. "Hi."

"Hello." She met him on the porch.

"Thanks for coming by." Bastian kissed her on the cheek. He smelled wonderful and looked even better in his beige T-shirt and jeans, but grimness showed on his face.

"What's wrong? You look upset."

He released a long exhale. "My grandma was making breakfast this morning and spilled orange juice on the floor. While she was mopping up, she slipped and banged her injured knee."

"Oh no. Does she need to go back to the hospital?"

"No. Dr. Kyle came by and examined her. She gave Gran a crutch to use, but she wants her to stay off her leg as much as possible. She's also concerned about her returning to the store too soon, and recommended she not go back for at least three weeks. But of course, all my grandma is worried about is the store." As he massaged the back of his neck, he gave Layla a rueful smile. "Sorry. I didn't mean to unload on you like that."

Layla could relate to his frustration. When Grandma Ruby had been in a car accident a couple of years ago and injured her leg, she'd been stubborn about sitting still.

Holding back on saying too much that might reveal her connection to Ruby, Layla rested her hand on his arm. "I understand. You're just concerned about her. Since the meeting is canceled, I'm free. Would it be helpful if I worked at the store today? I don't mind."

"I appreciate the offer, but the meeting's not canceled. The other thing she's concerned about is

Eden's wedding dress. With you here talking to her about it, there's a chance she'll stay in bed."

"Okay." She was willing, but Charlotte might be in too much pain to really concentrate. "I was hoping to borrow a laptop or a tablet to show her a few possibilities I found."

"Not a problem. She has a tablet and I have my laptop. Which one is better for you?"

"Let's go with her tablet. That way Charlotte will have the information, and she can bookmark the sites that catch her attention."

"That works." He let her walk ahead of him inside the house. "It's already upstairs with her."

As Layla followed him up the stairs, she took a deep breath. It would all go smoothly. Wouldn't it?

At the end of the wood-floored hall, Bastian knocked on the partially closed door before walking inside. "Gran, Layla's here."

Inside the room, ornate mahogany-wood furnishings leaned toward a Victorian style of decor. But instead of dark hues, sand-colored upholstery covered the wide headboard and matched the comforter and sheets partially turned down on the empty bed. Light beige and coral accent pillows were piled to one side.

In front of a sliding door leading to a balcony, Charlotte sat in one of two beige side chairs. Dressed in pink satin pj's, she had both feet propped on a wide, tufted square ottoman. Her toes were painted the same color as her pajamas and a pair of beige-and-pink slipper shoes, made popular by the Duchess of Sussex, sat on the floor beside her.

As Bastian looked from a metal crutch by the bed to his grandmother, he released a heavy breath.

Charlotte stared back at him with a defiant expression. She shifted her attention to Layla. "Hello."

Before leaving Atlanta, Layla had looked for a recent picture of Charlotte online and found one on Buttons & Lace's website.

It had been hard to reconcile the woman smiling warmly in the photo as the one Grandma Ruby had run into at the airport in Chicago. Rave reviews, including one from the actress Chloe Daniels, had touted her caring and professional demeanor.

Although Charlotte had light blue eyes, silvery blond hair and a fair complexion, Bastian's resemblance to her was evident. It was in their steady gazes and the innate self-assuredness that emanated from both of them.

"Hello." Layla shook hands with Charlotte.

Charlotte pointed to the chair across from her. "Bastian, bring it closer so Layla can sit next to me."

He complied. "Where's your computer tablet? Layla has some dresses to show you."

"It's on the bedside table with my glasses." Charlotte looked to Layla. "Would you like something to drink—tea, coffee, orange juice?"

"No, thank you." Layla sat in the chair.

Bastian handed Layla the tablet and gave Charlotte her glasses. "Are you comfortable? Do you need a pillow for your leg?"

"I'm fine." Charlotte patted his arm.

His gaze encompassed Layla and his grandmother

but lingered on Layla a bit longer. "Let me know if you need anything."

As he exited the room, Charlotte's attention settled on Layla. "My grandson told me I have you to thank for still having Poppy and Eden's business."

Layla wasn't sure how to respond. *You're welcome* didn't seem appropriate. "The dresses were there—I just thought I could help."

"Tell me more about this dress you sketched out. Bastian said you made it based on what Eden said she wanted?"

"Yes. The ideas were actually pulled from the dresses she tried on. I brought an updated drawing." Layla handed Charlotte the new sketch.

Charlotte put on her glasses. "You've added more detail to the lace on the sleeves and the skirt, but it's more delicate looking in this sketch."

Delicate was exactly what she'd been going for with the details of the lace. "I found two dresses that are close to it." Layla brought up the first website on her phone and sent it to the tablet. A window opened, and she handed the tablet to Charlotte.

"It's close," Charlotte said. "But the neckline is wrong. Eden specifically said she didn't want a V neckline."

"Oh—I didn't know that. Well, then the second one might be better." Layla pulled up the next site and sent it to the tablet.

Charlotte shook her head. "No. This skirt is more of an A-line. In your sketch, your skirt is slimmer.

And neither one of the dresses you showed me would work with that type of train."

Layla's heart sank. "I'll keep looking. Is it possible for me to search the online vendor catalogs that you have access to? I'll probably find better options."

"You won't find this exact dress. And now that you've raised Eden's hopes up and Poppy's expectations, they won't settle for less. This dress has to be sewn to the specifications of your drawing. But I can't do that on my own."

As Layla stared at the brace on Charlotte's wrist, the weight of the situation sank her down in the seat. She could keep searching during the time they had left. Maybe she would find something.

Or there was one other solution. Even as Layla considered it, she had reservations. But leaving this undone felt worse.

"What if I help you make the dress?"

"Can you sew?"

"I'm proficient. And I've assisted with making formal gowns and dresses."

Uncertainty remained on Charlotte's face. "Let's say you can sew well enough to help me. Eden's wedding is a month and a half away. Are you willing to put in the time and focus it's going to take to complete the dress by then?"

"Charlotte is going to regret trusting her reputation to a stranger..."

"You drew the dress of my dreams. I need your help to make it a reality..."

"You have to. I know you can fix this..."

Poppy's threat along with Eden's and Tyler's expectations swam in Layla's mind. Along with the assurances she'd given her grandma about alleviating her concerns.

She couldn't just go to the beach and drink cocktails, knowing that instead of fixing a problem she'd created more of them.

The type of guilt she'd experience letting so many people down would haunt her.

Layla gave the only answer she could. "Yes, I'm willing to dedicate my time and stay until the dress is done."

"But why do you want to do this? You're not from here? You don't know me or Eden."

"It's the right thing to do."

Charlotte held her gaze during the silence. "Okay, I'll take the chance. But I want at least one reference. You mentioned you had experience making formal gowns and dresses. Where was that?"

Layla almost said at Sashay Chic. "With a private label designer in California. I can get a reference from them. But I don't have their contact information with me right now. Can I give it to you later?"

Kinsley would vouch for her, but she'd have to tell her why first.

"Of course. Just pass it along to Bastian. He'll make the call."

"Thank you."

"The person you should be thanking is him. He trusts you, and I trust his instincts. He said he believes you genuinely want to help."

Hearing Bastian trusted her brought happiness to Layla, but also a hint of guilt. But she hadn't lied to him. She just hadn't expanded on certain things about herself.

"Let's get started." Charlotte took her legs off the ottoman and handed the computer tablet to Layla. "I need to evaluate your skills. There's a sewing machine down the hall. You can show me what you can do."

Did she mean like a sewing test? "You want to do it now?"

"Yes. Every minute counts."

"Are you supposed to be moving around? Bastian said—"

"The room isn't a mile away. It's just down the hall. Look, if we're going to work together, you're going to have to stick to two important rules. Don't fuss over me. And don't tattle on me to Bastian. Can you do that?"

Tattling wasn't Layla's style, but she wasn't on board with helping Charlotte keep secrets from Bastian. But what choice did she have?

Layla got the crutch by the bed and handed it to her. "I can."

Chapter Fifteen

Layla hovered close to Bastian's grandmother as they made their way toward the other room.

Halfway down, Charlotte teetered. Just as Layla reached out to grab her, she found her balance.

They continued, and the way Charlotte wielded the crutch—like an annoyance that prevented her from getting there faster—made Layla wince.

Finally, they reached their destination, and Layla released a pent-up breath.

Charlotte opened the door. "This is where we'll work together."

Layla walked farther in. "Oh, this is lovely."

Sunlight shining through large picture windows bathed the space in natural light. The brass candelabra chandelier hanging from the middle of the ceiling was equally eye-catching.

Bench seats with an assortment of tan and pink pillows lined the far wall. A worktable sat off to the side.

A female dressmaker's mannequin stood in front of three large floor-to-ceiling mirrors along the other side wall. The two end panels were on guide rails that allowed them to lay flat or swing out from the wall creating a three-way mirror.

Near the door, built-in shelves with neatly stacked fabric and spools of thread added splashes of color.

In the middle of the room an L-shaped table sat on a pale pink rug. The table housed a sewing machine in the longer section, and a serger on the adjoining smaller one.

The familiar scents of new textiles and scented fabric sizing spray wafting in the air awakened a childhood memory. An image of Grandma Ruby and her mother draping and pinning fabric on a dressmaker's mannequin emerged in Layla's mind.

For a brief moment, it was as if she could smell the satin fabric mixed with her mother's Joy perfume and peppermint candy.

Years ago, before Grandma Ruby had completely kicked the habit, she'd used the candy to curb the urge to smoke a cigarette. Or to cover up that she'd snuck one in.

The workroom where they'd collaborated at Sashay Chic's flagship store in Atlanta looked nothing like Charlotte's sewing room. But the workroom she remembered and Charlotte's space had the same layers of uniqueness, vibrancy and creative intimacy that reflected the women who worked in them.

Charlotte pointing to the table pulled Layla from the memory. "I assume you're familiar with both of these machines?"

"Yes, I am." The sewing machine was almost like the one Kinsley had in California. "This is the latest model, isn't it?"

"It is. I just got it a couple of months ago, and I love it. It's a time-saver, especially with the mending and minor alterations I do on the side for a few of my best customers."

Layla followed her gaze to the rolling garment rack with an assortment of clothing near the shelves of fabric.

Charlotte walked to a beige-and-white wingback chair tucked in the corner next to a small round table. "I set up the machine the other day to mend the blue pants on the rack, but I didn't get around to it. Start with them. Oh, and hand me the tablet, please."

Layla gave it to her.

After familiarizing herself with the sewing machine, she took the pants from the rack and settled into a modern beige leather chair with wheels in front of the sewing machine.

The inner seam had come undone on one of the pant legs. Lining up the start of the tear under the needle, she eased down on the pedal as she guided the fabric. It was like a walk in the park.

Once the repair was done, she brought the pants to Charlotte.

"Nice straight stitches. That's good." Charlotte handed the pants back to her. "Go ahead and fix the hem on the white blouse."

"Which one? There are two of them."

"The one toward the middle of the rack. You should find the thread you need for the machine in the top drawer on the left side of the table."

Layla hung up the pants and found the blouse. An area of the hem had separated.

The fabric was semi-sheer and lightweight. Sewing it on the machine would make the repair noticeable. Hand stitching it was a better choice.

And from the way Charlotte glanced up from the tablet and studied her, she probably knew that. This was definitely a test.

Searching through the drawer, Layla unearthed scissors, a needle and the right type of thread.

She secured the thread on the inside fold of the hem with a small knot.

"Make a small stitch, catching just a few threads of the fabric. Then make a longer stitch on the inside fold…"

Every time she sewed a basic blind stitch, she heard those instructions from her mom like a whisper in her thoughts. It was comforting. A reassurance that she was doing it right.

But she couldn't remember when the lesson had occurred. Maybe she really wasn't remembering her mother's teachings at all. Maybe she just wanted it to be her guiding voice.

"Who taught you how to sew and design clothing?" Charlotte asked.

Staying as close to the truth was the best way to go, wasn't it? Layla made another stitch. "My mother and my grandmother made outfits for people—friends, family."

One of the first lines in Sashay Chic's employee manual was to treat first-time customers like valued new friends and returning customers like family.

"Oh? Where did they do that?"

"Atlanta."

"Small world. My former business partner lives in Atlanta."

Layla mentally kicked herself. She should have chosen some obscure town just outside of the city. Hopefully, Charlotte wouldn't ask her if she'd heard of Sashay Chic or Ruby Morris.

Charlotte peered closely at the tablet screen. "That's interesting…"

Was she googling Sashay Chic or Grandma Ruby? Was she googling her? All of the places on social media where family pictures might exist flashed in Layla's mind.

The needle grazing her finger on the next stitch made her flinch. She held her breath, praying she hadn't drawn blood and that Charlotte hadn't discovered something incriminating.

But Charlotte didn't elaborate on what she'd found intriguing.

Layla breathed a little easier and finished the blouse. When she was done, she showed it to Charlotte.

"This is good work." Charlotte studied the front and the back of the hem. "Your mother and grandmother taught you well. What about measuring fabric, creating patterns, other alteration techniques, are you familiar with those things as well?"

"I am."

"Good. I still want to see you do some finishing work on the serger. But take a look at this. I jotted down a plan. I prefer to have all the details laid out before starting something new."

Layla rolled over the chair from the sewing station and sat down.

Charlotte showed her the list on the tablet. "First, we need to confirm Eden's measurements. With all the stress she's been under, they might have changed, and we want the most accurate numbers. Then we'll make a muslin. Do you know what that is?"

"Yes. It's a test garment that will allow us to check the fit of the dress before we make it."

It added a step to the dressmaking process, but it had been Grandma Ruby's preference when making an intricate custom design.

Charlotte went down the list. The way she organized the steps for making the dress was also similar to how Grandma Ruby had set up her plans.

But where Grandma Ruby had explained things in broad strokes and notes that sometimes only she understood, Charlotte's instructions were detailed and clear.

Their similarities had probably allowed them to work well together. But what about their contrasts?

Grandma Ruby feeling comfortable making decisions with a broader view could have seemed reckless to Charlotte. And Charlotte's need to have all the details could have been interpreted as hesitation by Grandma Ruby.

Layla mulled over the possibility.

Basic differences often led to disagreements. And in a tense situation, those differences could seem insurmountable.

Did this have anything to do with driving Charlotte and Ruby apart?

An hour later, Layla walked out of the house in a daze, her head overloaded with the intricacies of sewing the dress.

The floral motif for the train would take the most work. It required hand cutting flower and leaf embellishments from a piece of lace then painstakingly stitching them into a more intricate design on the tulle train. They also had to find a source for the specialty lace.

But first, they had to make the test garment. They would start that on Monday. The garment would also prove to Poppy that the dress could be made.

On the way to the car, Layla mentally ran through her schedule. The entire dressmaking process would take longer than the two weeks of vacation time she'd planned.

Naomi would probably be willing to watch over

her business for two and a half weeks, maybe three. After that she'd have to start teleworking. How long could she do that? Maybe a couple of more weeks? She'd also have to come up with an excuse for being away so long. A special project for a client might not raise too much suspicion with her dad and Patrice. But Tyler…

Layla's phone chimed in her purse, and she answered it. "Hello."

"Hello, Miss I'm-on-Vacation."

Caught off guard to hear her sister's voice, Layla stopped walking. They weren't twins, but her sister seemed to have some sixth sense about when she was on her mind.

"Tyler—this isn't your number."

"No, it is not. I'm on my way to lunch with a friend. The battery on my phone died so I'm borrowing his. We were just talking about you."

"Why?"

"Why do you think? Is the problem fixed?"

"Not yet, but it will be."

"How much longer is it going to take?"

Layla released a breath. Tyler and twenty questions. She didn't have the energy for it. "I have no idea how long it's going to take. But I won't get anything done if you keep bugging me."

"Bugging you? How is calling you today about something you said would be done yesterday bugging you? I get that you're on the beach, but some of us have more pressing issues than putting on more sunscreen."

"That's not fair. I had to change my vacation plans to fix your problem."

"How? Doing what?"

"Tyler… You just have to trust me."

"Great. Grandma's keeping secrets and now you are, too. I thought you were on my side."

The hurt in Tyler's voice got to her. "I am. If I could tell you what's going on, I would, but I can't."

"Well, when you finally decide to let me in on the big secret that's devastating my career, call me."

"Tyler—"

Her sister hung up.

Layla found the number, planning to phone her back. But what was the point? Like she'd tried to explain, she couldn't tell Tyler anything. And knowing her sister, she probably wouldn't answer the call anyway.

Helpless frustration made Layla close her eyes. Tyler would forgive her once the problem was fixed. Right now, she needed a job reference.

As she opened the car, she called Kinsley. Expecting to get her voice mail, Layla was relieved when she picked up. "Hey, Kins, it's me. How are you?"

"Excellent as of five minutes ago. I just won a new contract."

Layla dropped her things on the driver's seat. From the happiness in Kinsley's voice, it was easy for her to imagine her friend's light brown face and green eyes lit up with a smile.

Kinsley worked as a freelancer developing IT

systems. She usually took on short-term contracts during the year, which allowed time for her to make dresses.

"Congrats."

"Thanks."

Movement at the door of the cottage caught Layla's eye.

Bastian jogged down the stairs from the porch. He went to his truck parked nearby. After opening the back, he lifted the front of his shirt and wiped his face.

As her mind filled in the details of his exposed torso, her mouth dried out.

Bastian removed what looked to be paint cans from the bed of the truck. Before heading back inside the cottage, he glanced her direction.

Layla turned away and leaned on the front passenger side door.

Kinsley called out to her from the phone. "Are you still there?"

"I am. Sorry. Did you say something?"

"I asked how your vacation is going. You sound funny? Are you okay?"

"Just a little overwhelmed?"

"Why? You're not in your office."

"No, I'm not in my office." Layla toed a small pebble with the front of her shoe. "But I'm working a side job outside of accounting for a few weeks."

"You're joking."

"I'm not." But on some level, she wished she was.

"Are you in some type of financial trouble?"

"No. It's nothing like that, but…"

As good as it would feel to unburden herself to Kinsley, she couldn't break her promise not to tell Grandma Ruby's secret.

"I can't explain why." Layla nudged another pebble closer to the first. "At least not yet. I need a favor."

"What is it?"

"Someone is going to call you for a reference about my seamstress abilities. I told them I work for you. And they're probably assuming my employment with you was more than one week out of the year. And please don't mention that I'm an accountant or that my family owns Sashay Chic."

Kinsley's extended pause filled the silence. "Promise me you're not in danger."

"I'm not in danger. I'm perfectly fine."

Layla nudged the pebbles away. She was fine. Except for the nagging feeling that she might be jumping into the deep end.

"Who's going to call me?"

"A guy."

The sound of Bastian's footfalls echoed. Moments later he stood in front of her.

As she looked up and met his gaze, Layla's heart skipped beats.

Kinsley's eyes skewed more toward blue. His reminded her of the farmland she'd spotted on the drive that morning—green grass and amber-colored earth. He even smelled like it—in a very good way.

"Is he with you now?" Suspicion filled Kinsley's voice.

"He is."

"Put him on. I'll give him the reference."

"This probably isn't a good time to talk to him."

Bastian's brow quirked with a questioning expression.

"Do you need a reference or not?"

"Hold on." She put the phone on mute and spoke to Bastian. "Your grandmother asked me to give you the contact info for a reference. They're on the phone. She has a busy schedule and wants to give it to you now."

He shrugged. "Okay. Put us on speaker."

Layla unmuted the call and tapped the speaker icon. "Kinsley, he's here."

"Hello, my name is Kinsley Mitchell." Kins used her business voice. "I understand you need a reference for Ms. Price."

Bastian leaned toward the phone. "I do."

"What would you like to know?"

"During the time of her employment with you, was she a good employee?"

"Define good."

Bastian stared into Layla's eyes. "Was she punctual?"

"She was."

"Did she produce good quality work?"

"Always."

The wind blew a strand of hair on Layla's face.

As she reached up to smooth it out of her eyes, Bastian did, too.

She let him do it. The gentle brush of his fingers along her forehead left tingles.

"My impression of her is that she cares about people. She's not afraid to get her hands dirty, and she always finishes what she starts. Would you say that's accurate?"

"Yes, that's a very accurate impression. No matter what it takes, she'll complete the task."

Bastian's fingers lingered on her cheek, and Layla closed her eyes, fighting the urge to lean into him. "Would you hire her again?"

He dropped his hand from her face, and Layla immediately missed his touch.

"In a heartbeat," Kinsley replied. "I should confess, she was such a valued employee, I plan to keep tabs on her. Personally and often. Just in case she's changed her mind about her present work situation and would like to return to my employment. But I'm sure you understand the importance of treating your staff correctly."

Oh no... Kinsley was straying a little too far from her ex-boss role. "Thank you, Miss Mitchell. I appreciate you taking this call."

"You're welcome. Good luck with your new employment. And keep in touch."

"Uh...sure. Thanks again." Layla ended the call.

He chuckled. "It sounds like your former boss might hunt me down if you're not treated right."

"Was it that obvious? Sorry."

"Don't be. It's great that you have a friend that cares about you that much." He loosely took her hand. "Now would you mind telling me why my grandmother needed you to provide a reference."

That's right. He didn't know the outcome of the meeting. "None of the dresses I found will work so your grandmother and I are making Eden's dress together. Basically, I'm like your grandmother's apprentice. I know you're concerned about her resting. I'll do most of the work."

"Honestly, this could be the ideal situation. She'll be at home instead of the store, and she won't be moving around too much. But you don't look happy about it."

"Your grandmother really knows her stuff. Assisting her feels a little daunting."

Bastian brushed his thumb over the back of Layla's hand. "She does know her stuff. But it says a lot that she's willing to work with you. After being burned by her business partner, she usually prefers to work alone."

Hearing him describe what he believed happened back then echoed the unfairness Grandma Ruby had described to her about Charlotte's point of view. But now that she'd met Charlotte, she wanted to know more about her. And to understand more about what happened decades ago. But she couldn't allow herself to get too distracted. She had too many expectations to meet.

Bastian tightened his grasp. "What can I do to make this easier for you?"

The temptation to lean on him for comfort was so strong, it was hard to resist. He wanted to help, but he had no idea how complicated her circumstances were right then. And she couldn't explain.

The only thing she could do was make things less difficult on herself. And him.

When it came to balancing things in her life, she'd learned a long time ago, there was no such thing as squeezing in more. It was simple addition and subtraction. Saying yes to making the dress meant she had to give up something else.

Layla lifted her hand to Bastian's chest and stepped closer.

The corners of his eyes crinkled with the start of a sexy smile. "You sure you want to be close to me? I'm sweaty."

"I'm sure." Holding lightly onto the front of his shirt, she pressed her mouth to his.

Bastian slid his arms around her waist and she wound hers around his neck.

As the kiss deepened, the desire she felt for him swelled inside of her. But bittersweetness crept in, and the happy anticipation of more of anything with him deflated with one hard thump of her heart.

Layla pressed herself against Bastian, soaking in how good it felt to be with him like this.

A long moment later, she slid her arms from around Bastian and stepped away.

"I have to tell you something." Swallowing past tightness in her throat, she looked up at him. "That was our last kiss."

Chapter Sixteen

Bastian stretched a section of blue painter's tape above the baseboard in the guest cottage living room.

Void of furniture and with every window blind pulled up, the beige-tiled, white-walled space was filled with light.

The impressive sunny view of the surrounding lawn, the trees and the neighbors' fields had caused him to pause and look more than once throughout the morning and afternoon. Instead of flooding the room with music from his phone, he'd opened a window, letting in the sound of the birds and the gentle breeze.

Since he'd arrived in town ten days ago, he'd made good progress on painting the rooms and making repairs.

His phone buzzed and chimed on the black granite

counter separating the living room from the kitchen. Recognizing the ringtone, he barely glanced at the screen before answering the call. "Hi, Gran."

"Hello—can you come to the house?"

Bastian turned and rushed out the door. Had she fallen again? "I'm on my way. What's wrong?"

"One of the mirror panels in my sewing room isn't working right."

Urgency faded and he slowed down. His heart rate did the same. "I'll be over in a minute to take a look."

After doubling back for the toolbox, Bastian headed to the house.

He shouldn't have assumed something was wrong. But after his grandmother's second fall in the kitchen, it was hard not to feel concerned about her. He'd worry less when she healed up from her injuries.

Remaining busy kept him from hovering over her. If he had started doing that, his gran would probably whack him with the crutch that she found a million and one reasons not to use.

But at least she wasn't trying to work at Buttons & Lace.

Between shortening the store's operating hours and Layla volunteering to help, along with Darby working part-time, he'd been able to cobble together a work schedule.

On the weekdays, Layla opened the shop at ten, but she usually went in earlier to use the sewing machine in the office.

Darby started her shift around one and left when

he got there at four. He closed at six, handled the cleanup and made the night deposit.

The one task he hadn't been able to pry from his grandma's hands was the bookkeeping. Layla had volunteered to pitch in with that, too. She was familiar with the apps being used to organize the store's finances, but his gran had insisted on doing it.

Where was Layla? After her shift at Buttons & Lace ended, she usually came there to work with his grandma. But her car wasn't in the driveway.

Inside the house as he walked up the stairs, he listened for the sounds of his grandma and Layla.

The other day, when he'd come in to make a sandwich for a late lunch, they'd been so quiet, he'd peeked in on them to make sure they were okay.

His gran had been inspecting the bodice of the cotton test garment on the mannequin.

Layla had stood at the worktable cutting fabric.

They'd both been so engrossed in what they were doing, they hadn't noticed him. He'd started to say something but interrupting their companionable silence had felt wrong.

From what he'd noticed, they were getting along. And that was a good thing, considering his gran's hesitancy to work with anyone. But he wasn't surprised Layla had already put her at ease. Even though Layla was reluctant to talk about herself, he sensed her honesty, and that she genuinely cared about making the dress.

That's why he hadn't pushed back that day when Layla had told him that was their last kiss, and they shouldn't be involved with each other. He didn't agree with her claim that the two of them being together would complicate things. But he respected her wanting to stay focused on helping his grandmother.

Steps from the sewing room, his heart knocked in his chest as he mentally prepared himself.

He would stick to what he'd done the few times he'd been in the same space with Layla. Say hello. Smile. And pretend that every fiber of his being wasn't tuned into her voice, the smell of her perfume. Her just being there.

Bastian crossed the threshold.

His grandma stood in front of the mirror on the left, balancing on the crutch.

A four-step folding ladder was opened next to her.

His breath of relief and disappointment at not seeing Layla was replaced by a huff of concern. "I know you're not considering doing what I think you are."

"What?"

"Climbing up on this." Bastian dropped his toolbox on the top step of the ladder.

"I just got it out of the hall closet a minute ago because I knew you needed it." Guilt more than innocence reflected in his gran's wide-eyed expression.

He slid the mirror back and forth on the guide rail. "It's wobbly."

"The second wheel on the top bracket is loose."

Bastian put his toolbox on the floor then climbed the stepladder. "You're right. But how did you know it was the second wheel? You can't see that from down there."

She shrugged. "Lucky guess. And while you're up there, check the screws in the guide rail, too. There might be some missing."

Bastian deleted images of how her "lucky guess" had most likely played out before she'd called him. And he wasn't going to think about how she'd gotten the ladder into the room in the first place.

After finding the right screwdriver in his box, he got to work.

Instead of the cotton test garment, lighter fabric pinned in the shape of a bodice was on the mannequin. "How are things going with the dress?"

"Eden tried on the muslin a few days ago, and we only had to make a few adjustments to the pattern. Even Poppy was pleased. Layla started cutting the pieces for the dress this morning at the store. She's fast and efficient."

"Is she still there?"

"No, she was here. But right after I mentioned calling you about the mirror, she said she needed to run an errand." His grandma peered up at him. "Did you two have an argument?"

"No. Why would you ask that?"

"You've been avoiding coming here when she's around. Now she's avoiding you. If you didn't have a fight, what happened?"

Their kiss in the driveway popped into his thoughts along with Layla telling him it was their final one. If he would have known that was the case, he would have made it last a lot longer.

Bastian finished tightening the wheel. "Nothing really."

"So the two of you just had a hookup?"

"What? No." Bastian lost his grip on a screw, and it bounced on the floor. "Why are even using that term?"

"Don't look so shocked. I know all about hookup culture."

And I really didn't need to know that. He climbed down and picked up the screw. "Gran, all you need to know is that Layla and I are not together anymore. I wanted to move forward from where we started, but she said she couldn't. Her circumstances are complicated."

That was one of the reasons Layla had given him, along with wanting to avoid distractions.

"And what did you say when she told you that?"

"What could I say? I told Layla I respected her decision."

His gran nodded. "Okay. That was good, but do you know what you should have said?"

Was she really trying to give him dating advice? "Nope. I have no idea."

"You should have told her that you understand and that you can handle complicated. That's what the guy on this reality show I was watching featuring couples said when the woman he was interested in mentioned her life was complicated."

And of course everything that occurred on those types of shows was true.

He held back a smile and the urge to tell her to

sit down. She looked relaxed and rested. And she'd never been this chatty with him about his personal relationships.

Bastian dug out more screws in his toolbox. "What happened to you telling me not to get involved with women who were trouble?"

She pointed at him. "Oh no, that's still true. Trouble is messy, but complicated can just mean things are a little tangled up in Layla's life." His grandmother shrugged. "Who hasn't experienced that? Understanding requires patience. And if she knows you have that, then she'll worry less about whether you can handle being with her."

That actually made sense.

As his grandmother walked to the recliner, Bastian climbed back up the stepladder and filled in the missing screws on the guide rail. "Has Layla talked to you about herself?"

"Not really. She did mention that her mother and grandmother were the ones who taught her how to sew. But she turned sad when she mentioned them. I think they passed away."

"That's rough." Was she alone and without family?

"You met her before I did. What did you learn about her? Or was there no talking involved?"

A tiny bit of heat crept up his neck into his ears. Nope. He didn't care how much she'd learned about casual relationships. He wasn't going there with her.

"I know she has a friend named Kinsley who really cares about her. Pretzels are her favorite snack, and she likes zombie movies."

Except maybe *Zombie Robot Soldier Beasts*.

The cute, incredulous look that had been on Layla's face when he'd told her about the movie flashed in his mind.

Bastian couldn't stop a chuckle.

His gran had gone silent. She stared at him with a soft smile on her face.

"What?" he asked.

"Are you done fixing my mirror."

"I am." He packed up his toolbox.

On his way out, he kissed her cheek. "See you later. I have to get ready to go to the shop."

"What are you going to do about Layla?"

Bastian paused at the door. "I don't know."

A couple of days later, Bastian parallel parked in front of the Bolan Book Attic.

He spotted Mace's red crew cab farther down.

They were meeting up for an afternoon run.

He got out of the truck.

Dressed in loose dark shorts, a white tank top and athletic shoes, the sun heated up his skin.

As he walked down the sidewalk, he couldn't stop his gaze from wandering to the other side of the town square and across the opposite street.

Two women carrying large boutique shopping bags walked out of Buttons & Lace.

It was just after one o'clock. Darby was there. Layla had probably already left for his grandmother's.

"You should have told her that you understood and that you could handle complicated..."

Since their talk the other day, his gran's suggestion kept coming into his mind. But it wasn't like he could suddenly walk up to Layla and say, "Hey, babe, it's all good, I'm into complicated."

Mace met Bastian on the sidewalk. Similar to Bastian, he wore athletic clothes suitable for a run.

He clapped Bastian on the back. "You ready?"

"Let's do this." Bastian tucked his phone in a band on his arm.

In need of another routine outside of the shop and looking after Charlotte, he'd started running with Mace three times a week.

After using a bench near the fountain for a light stretch, they jogged the paved path toward city hall.

As they veered onto a running trail shaded by trees, they joined other joggers and walkers.

Valuing companionship over conversation, they both played music through their earbuds. But into the first mile, Bastian barely registered the beat. His mind drifted back to Layla.

Their last kiss had felt like a reluctant goodbye. He'd thought she was just worried about making Eden's dress. He hadn't expected her to say they couldn't see each other.

But he also sensed that she was holding back on something. He just couldn't figure out what it might be. Was it something with her family? Another guy?

Noticing the space between him and Mace had widened, Bastian picked up the pace.

His thoughts of Layla were replaced by trying to block out the hard exhales and inhales searing through his lungs. But then his mind and his body shifted gears. The echo of his heartbeat. The soles of his trainers hitting the pavement. His breathing evening out with his stride, all became part of the rhythm that brought him close to peace.

Following a loop in the trail, they headed back to town, sprinting the final few yards.

Slowing to a walk, both of them were out of breath as they emerged from the trees near city hall.

"Good run." Mace grinned. "But the way you were lagging the first few miles, I thought you were tapping out."

"Five miles is an easy day. I was just distracted."

As they walked back to their trucks, Mace glanced over at him. "Everything okay with Charlotte and the shop?"

"She's getting around better, and despite the shorter store hours, business is good." Bastian wiped sweat from his brow.

Mace waited, clearly expecting him to say more.

It might help to talk to someone other than his grandmother. "It's Layla. Short version—we were together and now we're not."

"So the rumors were right. You two really were a thing."

"People were talking about us?"

"Yeah, just a few. Someone saw you two kissing

near Brewed Haven. You know how it is around here. But I'm sorry to hear you're not with her anymore. What happened? Did you have a fight?"

"No. Things were good." Bastian tucked his earbuds into a pocket on his armband. "Right up until the time she decided us being in a relationship was too complicated."

"When are relationships not complicated?"

"True, but I get where she's coming from. You probably heard she and my grandma are making Eden Ashford's dress. Layla's just trying to do the right thing. She wants to stay focused on work and not let the situation get twisted up in her personal life."

"That sounds familiar. Before Zurie and I got together, she felt the same way about her personal life and managing her commitment to Tillbridge."

"How did you change her mind?"

"Change her mind?" Mace chuckled. "No one changes Zurie's mind. But I did all I could to make the choice of us being together a much better proposition than us being apart."

As they paused by Bastian's truck, Mace's attention shifted.

Zurie came down the street. Her straight black hair fluttered over her shoulders with her purposeful stride. A version of Rina, her demeanor was more serious than her sister's.

But as she came closer, a radiant smile took over

as she mainly focused on Mace. "You two are done already?"

"Already?" Mace loosely wrapped an arm around her back. "We ran the entire trail."

"You made good time." Smiling, she glanced at Bastian. "You must be causing him to up his game."

"Possibly."

"Up my game?" Mace laughed. "So, you think I've been slacking off?"

"I didn't say that." She laid her hand on his chest.

"Careful. I'm sweaty," Mace cautioned.

"I don't care." She rose on her toes and gave Mace a brief kiss that turned into two.

Envy and longing pinged faintly in his chest. Bastian shifted his attention to taking the band from his arm.

He and Layla had said almost the exact same thing to each other standing in his grandma's driveway, but their kiss hadn't ended in happy smiles.

"I'd better get going." Bastian turned to walk toward his truck. "Good to see you, Zurie. Mace—don't forget to text me about if we're running this weekend."

Zurie looked to Bastian. "You're joining us Saturday at the Starlight Tasting, right?"

"About that…" Mace's gaze briefly met Bastian's before sliding to Zurie. "I was going to mention that to him, but—"

"You forgot? I thought you might. That's why I've already taken care of it." Smiling, Zurie turned her attention to Bastian. "I talked to Layla. She'll explain the details. You're joining us at our private table at the event. And remind her that casual means casual. Date night is about having fun."

Chapter Seventeen

In Charlotte's sewing room, Layla circled the mannequin draped in a plain satin bodice and skirt that were pinned together.

Charlotte was nearby also inspecting the beginnings of the dress that would eventually have a lace overlay on the bodice.

A light breeze along with a faint revving sound came through an open window.

Layla glanced that direction. Was that Bastian pulling his truck into the driveway?

The revving sound turned into the steady drone of a lawn mower.

Shoot. It wasn't. Where was he? She really needed to talk to him before he went to Buttons & Lace that evening. The flyer about the Starlight Tasting was practically burning a hole in the back pocket of her jeans.

Zurie inviting her to sit with her and Mace at their group's private table at the event had been a nice, unexpected gesture. And she'd said yes, not realizing Zurie was extending the invite to her and Bastian as a couple. Then Zurie had mentioned that only couples would be sitting at the table because it was their date night.

She'd wanted to clear up the misconception about her and Bastian, but a few of the locals shopping in the store had joined in the conversation. From what the locals had said, they'd assumed she and Bastian were a couple, too.

"This area near the hip looks uneven." Charlotte maneuvered one of the pins, but her injured hand limited her dexterity.

The pin dropped to the bottom of the skirt.

"Darn this thing." Charlotte glared at the brace on her wrist. Favoring her good leg, she wobbled as she leaned down for the pin.

"I'll get it."

As Layla rose from picking the pin up, Charlotte reached out and held on to her arm to steady herself.

With her other hand, Charlotte smoothed past the edge of her oversize emerald shirt and rubbed over the thigh above her hurt knee. It looked slightly puffy underneath her leggings.

She sighed. "I'm useless."

"No, you're not. Don't say that." Layla put her

hand over Charlotte's. "This dress couldn't happen without you."

"Maybe. Maybe not." Charlotte slipped her hand away and hobbled to the leather chair by the sewing machine. She sat down. "You know what you're doing. I'm surprised you didn't follow in your mother's and grandmother's footsteps. Why didn't you?"

Layla fixed the area on the dress that Charlotte had pointed out. She had anticipated this type of question. The answer was simple.

"I'm not good enough. My mother and grandmother had real talent. The way they worked together was effortless. They would start on a dress, and in no time, it was done. The way it seemed to just show up on the mannequin in a few days was like magic."

A memory Layla hadn't thought of in a while, popped into her mind. She laughed. "When I was little, before I understood how dresses were made, I believed my mom and grandmother were like Cinderella's fairy godmother, and that when no one was looking, they waved magic wands and made the finished dresses appear."

Charlotte laughed. "I bet they loved that."

"Yeah, especially my mom. When I was eight years old, even though she knew I understood differently, one day she gave me a wand…"

The expanded recollection of standing in her childhood bedroom with a wand in her hand made Layla widen her smile. "She told me to close my eyes and wave it in the air. When I opened them, she was holding the prettiest blue Easter dress I'd ever seen. She'd made it for me."

"Oh, that's so wonderful. I bet you wore it all the time because it was your favorite dress."

"I..." A sting of sadness stole Layla's words.

She'd worn the dress only once. It was the last thing her mother had ever made for her.

"Oh no, did I say something wrong?" Charlotte rolled the chair closer. "I upset you."

"No, you didn't. I'm fine." Layla sniffed away the sudden stuffiness in her nose and blinked back the tears.

She didn't know Charlotte that well. What was she doing sharing such a personal memory with her?

As Layla busied herself with the dress, Charlotte's empathy-filled voice reached her. "I can only imagine how you feel. You must miss them a lot."

Miss them? Layla almost said her grandmother was still alive. But she did miss seeing her mom and grandmother working together.

She turned toward Charlotte. "I do miss them."

Charlotte limped over to Layla. "Do you mind if I give you a hug?"

The sincere request prompted Layla to open her arms. "No, I don't mind."

Charlotte embraced her. The comforting, motherly hug ended with a reassuring squeeze.

As Charlotte moved back, she gently grasped Layla's shoulders. "You say you're not good enough, but I'm sure if your mom and grandmother saw the dress you're creating now, they would be impressed with your talent."

Proud of her making a good effort, maybe, but impressed? No. Tyler was the impressive one.

What Charlotte was seeing in Eden's dress was beginner's luck fueled by a desperate attempt to fix a broken situation.

Charlotte leaned back a little more and studied her. "You don't believe me?"

"I didn't say that."

"You don't have to. I can see it in your face. Telling yourself you're not good enough is what's stopping you from seeing your talent. And now that I think of it, I probably need to take a dose of that medicine. Because telling myself I'm useless is causing me not to see what I can still do despite my injuries. Let's help each other out and make a pact. From this point forward, I'm not allowed to see myself as useless, and you aren't allowed to view yourself as not good enough."

What Charlotte said sounded straight out of the self-help books Tyler loved to read.

But the kindness in Charlotte's eyes made Layla hold back an objection. She nodded. "Okay."

"Good." Charlotte started to turn away but hesitated. "Can I share something else with you?"

"Sure."

"Sometimes, the moments we remember, especially the ones with the people we've lost, might feel bittersweet, but they serve a purpose. They remind us to make more good moments with the people we enjoy and care about."

Making more good moments was important, but to feel enfolded in the bond her mother and grandmother shared as they made one of their creations... Emotion started to well in Layla. She would give almost anything to feel that again.

Footfalls thumped on the stairs.

Sebastian? When had he come into the house?

Charlotte reached into the breast pocket of her shirt and pulled out a crumpled, clean tissue. She pressed it into Layla's hand. "If he asks about your eyes and why you sound a little stuffed up, tell him it's allergies."

Layla turned toward the mannequin and dabbed her eyes and nose. Not that Bastian would notice her face. Lately, he barely looked at her.

Yes, she'd asked that they cool things off, but she hadn't expected a distance the size of the Arctic Ocean to exist between them.

Sebastian walked into the room. "Hey, Gran."

Layla tossed the tissue in a nearby trash basket and faced them.

Sebastian was dressed in his running gear. His hair was mussed and looked slightly damp.

"Hello." As Charlotte lifted her face, he kissed her on the cheek. "If you're hungry, don't forget, there's still some of that baked chicken Philippa brought over yesterday in the fridge."

"Thanks. I'll have some before I leave for the store." Bastian looked to Layla. "Hello." His gaze narrowed with a slightly concerned expression. "Are you okay? Your eyes look red."

She cleared her throat. "Yes—allergies, I think."

He tipped his head toward the door. "Can we talk in the kitchen?"

"Sure, actually, I need to talk to you, too."

Charlotte smiled at Layla and Bastian as they left.

In the kitchen, Bastian took a glass from an upper cabinet. "Would you like some water?" He filled his glass from the dispenser inside the refrigerator.

"No, thank you. I'm good." She stood at the nearby counter.

"One of the neighbors is mowing his field. Is that what's kicking up your allergies?"

"That could be it."

"You said you needed to talk to me." He took a sip from his glass and his bicep flexed.

Over the past few days, she'd caught sight of him in everything from shorts to jeans to shirts that fit him oh so well. His fresh-from-a-workout look was one of her favorites. Even the faint smell of sweat wafting from him was appealing.

But knowing what existed underneath his clothes made the look-but-don't-touch restrictions she'd placed on herself, when it came to him, a cruel joke.

"I think there's been a misunderstanding. Today at the store, Zurie and I were talking about the Starlight Tasting at Tillbridge this Saturday. She invited me—us—to sit at her family's private table."

He joined her at the counter. "She told me after I finished running with Mace."

"Did she also mention it's date night for their group? We're probably being invited because people think we're a couple. I wanted to explain that we weren't, but she was in a hurry, and there were people in the store. It just wasn't the right time."

"I didn't say anything either. But I was thinking you should go. You're already staying at Tillbridge. It's just a short walk for you."

It wasn't surprising to hear him say that, but it felt wrong. "I think you should go. They're your friends. I'm sure they're all looking forward to seeing you."

"But were you interested in going?"

"Yes. But if I weren't here, is it something you would have gone to?"

Bastian shrugged. "Probably. The event has food."

Food? That was typical guy reasoning. She coughed behind her hand, trying to suppress a laugh.

He cocked his head to the side. "Are you laughing at me?"

"No."

A small smile played on his lips. "Yes, you are, and I deserve to know why."

"It's nothing, really. It was just how you answered my question. The event has food."

"Food is important." As he put down his half-empty glass, he flashed a boyish grin.

It reminded Layla of the one he'd given her when he'd scored junk food at the motel.

The recollection made her smile. "You're right. It is."

A look came into his eyes as if he was remembering something. His smile started to dim.

Was he thinking about that night at the motel, too? Had the memories already turned bittersweet?

Bastian fiddled with his glass on the counter. "We could rock-paper-scissors for it, or flip a coin?"

As he glanced up, teasing was in his eyes, and she had to smile. "We could."

Or they could both enjoy a good moment like Charlotte had told her earlier.

Layla slid her hand forward but stopped short of touching his. "Or we could go to the event as friends. We really don't have to elaborate on our status unless it comes up."

He looked at her as if he was mulling the idea over. "Alright, we'll go as friends."

Chapter Eighteen

Twinkles of light and a partial moon shone in the dark blue canopy of the sky above the pavilion—a social oasis on the edge of the pasture at Tillbridge Stables.

Laughter and conversation reverberated as adults of all ages danced in front of the live band playing under the covering. A singer with the vocal range and presence of Jennifer Hudson owned the stage, performing eighties tunes to modern pop music.

In a large area in front of the pavilion, more people perused the booths bordering the tables on the grass. Restaurants and eating establishments, including the Brewed Haven Café and Pasture Lane Restaurant at Tillbridge, along with a winery, farms and artisans located in or near the town of Bolan, provided food and must-haves for the sizable crowd.

Layla sipped a crisp chardonnay. The oaky, caramelized-apple flavor of the wine was a nice complement to the cherry-barbecue-sauced ribs and peach-glazed wings she'd tried from the Montecito Steakhouse.

Bastian, who sat next to her, ate ribs and chatted with Zurie, who sat on the other side of him.

Friends.

Agreeing to attend the event together as just acquaintances had sounded like a great idea a few days ago. But then he'd shown up looking so good. She couldn't blame the blonde two tables over for staring at him. The way his dark jeans and navy Henley hugged him in all the right places deserved a second look and possibly a third.

But friends didn't notice those things about each other. Or envy a drop of barbecue sauce.

Bastian listened to something Mace, who sat next to Zurie, was telling him. Laughing, he closed his lips over a spot of sauce on his thumb, sucking it away.

As if they had a mind and scintillating memories of their own, the peaks of her breasts tingled underneath her casual teal dress.

Trying to cool off her thoughts and ease the dryness in her throat, she sipped more chardonnay.

Bastian leaned toward her as he cleaned his hands with a towelette. "Mace wants to introduce me to some people he works with." His gaze narrowed in question on her face. "You okay?"

"I'm fine." Thankfully, he couldn't read her mind. "Have fun."

I'll just sit here in couples' land and pretend it isn't hella-awkward.

And doing that was about as easy as not noticing Bastian.

Layla glanced at her tablemates. As if they'd read the same memo, the guys were dressed in jeans and pullover shirts. She and the rest of the women had opted for more colorful outfits.

To her left, Rina glowed with happiness in a yellow dress, resting her head on the shoulder of her muscular, blond-haired fiancé, Scott.

The stunt coordinator had flown in that morning, back from his latest movie gig. The supervisors and staff of the café had surprised Rina, volunteering to cover Brewed Haven's booth so she could spend the entire night with him.

Rina and Zurie's cousin Tristan Tillbridge, a former bull rider, and co-owner of the stable along with them, sat next to his beautiful, dark-haired wife, Chloe Daniels. Tyler would have definitely given the actress a ten for her simple yet elegant peach jumpsuit.

Tristan's beige Stetson checked the box for being on point. He wore it as easily as Chloe carried her celebrity status. Their Black power-couple vibe was strong, and anyone could see how devoted they were to each other.

Zurie, casual yet professional-looking in a sky blue dress, had been in sync with Mace, monitoring the flow of the event. He periodically checked in with security, and currently, she was conferring with the service staff. But earlier, when they'd been at the table, their focus had been on each other.

A pang of envy prompted Layla to down the rest of her wine. If she and Bastian had attended the event as a real couple, would they have held hands like Rina and Scott, or snuck in kisses whenever they could like Chloe and Tristan? Or would they have had the ease of just existing together as a couple like Zurie and Mace?

She'd never know.

The band announced they were taking a break.

Rina nudged her arm. "Scott's going to the booth for more wine. Do you want anything?"

"Would you bring me back another chardonnay, please?"

"Not a problem." Scott glanced to everyone else at the table. "I'm going to the vineyard booth. Anyone want anything?"

Chloe pointed to her half-full cup. "Merlot, if you don't mind."

"I want more of their fried mozzarella. You'll need a hand carrying everything." Tristan stood. "I'll go with you."

Chloe grasped Tristan's arm. "Bring back some olive dip if they have any left. And if the line isn't too long, can you bring back some honey-cinnamon cookies from the bee farm booth? They're near the one for the winery."

A hint of humor lit up his face. "Are you sure that's it?"

"No." She gave him a radiant smile. "I'd love a kiss when you get back."

He leaned in and briefly pressed his lips to hers. "One now. One later."

"Thank you." A smile remained on her face as Tristan and Scott walked away.

Rina shook her head. "And to think, when he was seven, he used to run from the girls in school who tried to kiss him."

"Aww." Chloe laughed. "I bet he was so cute. I was the same with boys. But instead of running, I used to just push them off the jungle gym."

"And that's why I love you." Rina opened her arms wide. "Get over here. You're too far away."

Their antics made Layla smile and think of Tyler. She actually missed her and her unannounced drop-ins at the office or her apartment. Tyler wasn't happy with her now, but she'd forgive her once the jinx situation was straightened out, wouldn't she?

As the willowy actress picked up her cup of wine and got up, two security personnel in dark pants and matching blue casual pullovers started to walk toward her. Realizing she was just joining Rina and Layla on the other side of the table, they remained in place.

As Rina hugged Chloe, she glanced at the security staff. "They're being extra vigilant. Is something up?"

"No." Chloe settled in the chair on the other side of Rina. "But with me and Dominic both being here, Mace suggested taking extra precautions. A few off-duty deputies are keeping an eye on us."

Across the area, Philippa Gayle, the chef of Pasture Lane Restaurant at Tillbridge, and Dominic Crawford, host of the popular cooking show *Farm to Fork with Dominic Crawford*, shared an L-shaped booth.

Security stood nearby monitoring the long line of people waiting for samples or to meet Dominic.

Rina glanced over Layla's shoulder. "Bastian and Mace look like they're in a deep conversation with the other deputies that are here. Is Bastian thinking of joining the sheriff's department?"

Layla glanced to where Bastian and Mace sat talking with a group at another table. "I don't know. He hadn't mentioned it to me."

"Typical." Chloe and Rina looked at each other as they said it at the same time.

"Guys and communication." Chloe shook her head. "I have to remind Tristan all the time that mind reading isn't my superpower."

"It's the same with Scott." Rina gave a subtle eye roll. "If Bastian is considering working for the sheriff's department, that would be good, right? You two wouldn't have to do the long-distance thing."

Chloe and Rina both waited for an answer.

Layla debated over what to say. "Well…"

"Oh no." Chloe's shoulders sank with disappointment. "Don't say you're the one who's not staying. We just met."

"Or did you two break up?" Rina asked.

Never skimp on shoes or tell a lie over a good glass of wine. Those were two of Tyler's golden rules. And it seemed like a good time to use them. She couldn't tell them everything, but she could give them an answer that was in the ballpark of the truth.

"It's both, actually. I'm not sure how long I'm staying in town. And Bastian and I, we're just friends."

Rina's brow raised. "I am so sorry. I shouldn't have assumed."

"Add me to that list." Chloe held up her hand. "I heard the same through the grapevine and believed it was true."

"We're the worst." Rina hung her head a moment and laughed. "Zurie made a huge deal about inviting you to date night. We should have just said we were welcoming you to town." She patted Layla's arm. "Don't worry. Just as fast as false rumors spread, the truth about you and Bastian not being together will eventually get out."

Chloe pointed. "It just did."

Layla glanced over her shoulder.

The blonde from two tables over was talking to Mace and Bastian near the bee farm booth. Laughing, she stepped closer and looked up at Bastian.

And he didn't move away.

He could talk to anyone he wanted. Like she'd just told Chloe and Rina, they weren't together.

Still, disappointment and regret drove Layla's gaze back to her cup of chardonnay. She took a long sip.

Never tell a lie over a good glass of wine... That rule left out an important consideration. What to do if the truth hurt.

Chapter Nineteen

"I thought I recognized you." The blonde, Noelle, laid her hand on Bastian's arm. "You've just started coming to the gym."

"Yeah, I have. Thanks to this guy." Subtly backing away from Noelle's hand, he turned more toward Mace.

Help me out. Bastian glanced at Mace, hoping he understood the look he was giving him. Noelle seemed nice, but he wasn't interested in getting to know her.

Mace nodded. "Just doing what I can to help." He pointed. "I need to take care of something."

Heck, yeah. "That's right." Bastian nodded back. "We do need to take care of that, don't we?"

"No, you don't. I got it." Mace backed away. "It

was nice meeting you, Noelle." Bastian caught a glint of humor in his eyes.

Not wanting to come off as rude, he turned his attention to Noelle. Once they progressed past workouts, the best protein shakes and the upcoming 5K in the next town, their conversation stalled.

The spark wasn't there like it had been when he'd first met Layla.

Noelle went back to her friends.

Bastian spotted Mace standing in line at the winery booth with Tristan and Scott. He really needed to talk to Mace about his wingman skills, or maybe Mace needed to lose his wingman card altogether.

As he joined the guys, Mace grinned. "So, are you taking Noelle out?"

Scott exchanged a questioning look with Tristan. "Noelle? What about Layla?"

"Hold up." Bastian waved them off. "No, I'm not taking Noelle out. And I'm not cheating on Layla. We're not together."

"Good to know." Tristan huffed a chuckle. "Otherwise, none of us would be able to go back to that table tonight. Make sure you explain the situation to Chloe, Zurie and Rina. They take this couples' night stuff seriously."

"I think the ladies are way ahead of us on that." Scott moved forward in line. "They've already introduced Layla to someone."

"What? Who?" Bastian looked to the table.

A dark-haired guy around their age leaned down and spoke to Layla.

"Isn't that the new lieutenant at the firehouse?" Tristan asked. "But isn't he engaged to a police chief's daughter?"

"Yep," Mace said. "She lives in the town where he moved from in Virginia. I heard he has a history of stepping out on her though. Bold move considering her daddy owns a gun."

Scott chuckled wryly. "That's probably why he transferred here. But I think Rina mentioned it's an on-and-off relationship."

A DJ started playing upbeat dance music in the pavilion.

The lieutenant held his hand out to Layla.

She took it and got up.

Curiosity and something else he couldn't explain sparked a strange burning sensation in Bastian's chest. "What's the current status of his relationship?"

Tristan moved forward in line behind Scott. "From his perspective, tonight it's off."

"Tonight?" Mace laughed. "Try every night. I've talked to him. His perspective is probably why the relationship isn't working out in the first place."

"I'll be right back." Bastian cut through the crowd.

He'd met guys like this lieutenant in the army, pretending they were free agents when technically they weren't. And in a small town, getting involved with a guy like him only led to problems. Layla didn't need that. He was just watching out for a friend.

As he reached the dance floor, "Electric Boogie" came on. The familiar beat and lyrics quickly pulled a crowd that practically forced him to follow the steps of the dance.

In front of him, Layla joined the lieutenant in one of the lines. Her movements were smooth and melodic as she danced the electric slide.

More people joined in, and the distance between the dancers closed.

A woman bumped Layla back into the lieutenant, and he caught her by the waist. And he took his sweet time letting her go.

The song blended into a country song, and couples started linking up for the two-step.

Bastian made his way to Layla and the lieutenant.

Smiling, Layla shook her head and told the guy, "I don't know this one."

"It's simple. I'll teach you." The lieutenant reached for her hand.

Bastian came up beside her. "Hey, guys. Sorry to interrupt." He looked to Layla. "Something important has come up. Can I talk to you for a minute?"

"Sure." She smiled at the lieutenant. "Thanks for the dance."

Layla walked in front of Bastian to an area off to the side. As she faced him, genuine concern filled her expression. "What's wrong? Has something happened to Charlotte?"

"No. It's about the lieutenant."

Her brow furrowed in confusion. "The lieutenant?"

"The one you were dancing with."

"You mean James?"

"Yeah, James. I was talking to the guys about him, and they said his priorities are screwed up. He's got an on-again, off-again relationship with his fiancée. He's not the type of guy you should get involved with."

"Oh, I shouldn't, huh?" Irritation simmered in Layla's eyes as she crossed her arms over her chest. "And what about the blonde? Did you get the play-by-play on her personal life or were you too busy butting into mine?"

"Hold on. Tha—"

"No, you hold on. I was dancing and having a good time with James. Not getting engaged to him. But I guess I was just supposed to sit at the table and watch you get handsy with the blonde." She cut him off with a look. "You know what. It doesn't matter. I'm going back to my room."

"Fine. I'll take you back." Maybe they could have a calmer conversation in the truck.

"No. I'll take the guesthouse shuttle." Layla spun on her heels and stalked off toward the parking lot.

What was up with her? She was overreacting. But there was no point in talking to her if she wouldn't listen to him.

Bastian went back to the table.

Everyone else had already returned to their seats.

"Where's Layla?" Rina asked.

He sat down. "She went back to the guesthouse."

"She left?" Chloe said. "But she looked like she was having a good time dancing with James. Did he do something wrong?"

Bastian faced their concerned frowns and puzzled looks along with the truth. He'd been the one to ruin Layla's night. "No. I did." He stood. "I need to talk to her."

In the gravel parking lot adjacent to the pasture, he searched for the guesthouse shuttle, but it wasn't there.

Jumping into his truck, he made the short drive to the guesthouse.

As he arrived in the parking lot, guests exited the shuttle.

Taking the first open parking space he could find, he got out, jogged up the stairs to the porch and through the entrance.

In the semicrowded lobby, he saw Layla getting on the elevator.

Damn. He'd just missed her. Spotting the door to the stairwell, he opened it and double-timed it up the stairs to the second floor.

Flying out the door, he caught a glimpse of Layla walking into her guest quarters on the right.

He didn't know the room number. If need be, he'd call Mace and beg Zurie to help him out. But he'd try another way first.

As Bastian walked down the hall, he phoned Layla. On the fifth ring, she answered. "Bastian…"

"I know you don't want to talk to me. But just give me one minute. And then I'll leave you alone."

"Your voice is echoing. Where are you?"

"Near your room. I don't know which one you're in."

The door he'd just passed opened, and Layla

stood in the threshold. She moved aside, indicating he should come in.

After shutting the door, Layla faced him. She no longer appeared angry, but gloominess shadowed her eyes.

His own disquiet settled in. Less than an hour ago, she'd been smiling and laughing. And he'd taken that from her because he'd chosen to be an ass.

"I was out of line talking to you about James. It was none of my business." He walked over to her. "And I also need you to know that I'm not that guy— the type who thinks I have a say in what you do just because we've spent time together."

Memories of being with Layla, holding her, kissing her, intermingled with images of her and James. "But I can't lie. I don't want to be your friend. But I respect what you're doing to help my grandmother and the shop. I think the best thing is for me to take off for Virginia earlier than I'd planned."

She nodded and crossed her arms almost hugging herself. "Okay. If that's what you think you need to do."

"If you're worried about keeping Buttons & Lace open, don't be. I was up-front with my grandmother from the beginning about maybe having to switch to a more abbreviated schedule until she could start working again, so she's aware."

"If that's what you want."

He turned and opened the door.

Her voice was so low he almost didn't hear it. "Goodbye, Sebastian Raynes."

She'd said his whole name. In a relationship, when you broke up with someone, and they said goodbye using your whole name, that was final. Once you walked away from each other there was no turning back.

But they weren't in a relationship. They hadn't even gotten the chance to be in one.

"No, Layla, that's not what I want." Bastian shut the door and turned back around. "I want complicated. In fact, I want all the complicated you got. I can handle it."

As he walked back over to Layla, he looked into her eyes that had gone wide.

"This might sound crazy because we haven't known each other that long, but I think we have something." Bastian held her gently by the shoulders. "I don't know what it is yet. But I do know it's special. And I'm not ready to walk away from it. And I think you feel the same way. If I'm right, just take a chance with me."

Her arms dropped, and misery came into her eyes. "There's so much you don't know."

"Are you married?"

"No."

"Is there a guy someplace waiting for you to come back to him?"

"No."

"Are you on the run because you've done something illegal?"

Her brow crinkled in confusion. "No, absolutely not."

"Then what I don't know can wait. What I do need to know, right now, is if you're willing to take a chance with me?"

Layla looked into Bastian's eyes and her heart overflowed with the desire to take that chance. But her mind was also filled with all that could go wrong.

Honestly, she wasn't entirely sure what to do. But just like he didn't want to be that guy, she didn't want to be that woman. The type who lets what she really wants slip from her grasp.

But she'd always finished what she started. She'd made a promise to Grandma Ruby and Tyler. She had to get them what they wanted. And if she couldn't, she needed to know in her heart that she did her best to clear every obstacle. That she grasped every opportunity. And that meant finishing Eden's dress.

Taking a chance with Bastian would mean asking him to take a huge blind leap of faith in trusting her now, and a promise that when the time came, she would tell him everything. And a confession that he might not like what he found out when she did.

Layla released a measured breath, hoping to calm her heart knocking on her rib cage. "I want to take a chance with you more than anything, but…" She closed her eyes, trying to find the words.

Bastian cupped her face and softly kissed her.

The feel of his lips on hers pulled out a sigh. Finally. That's what every part of her seemed to say in unison.

"Layla." The warmth of his mouth feathered over

her lips as his hands dropped to her waist. "We'll figure it out."

She rested her hands on his chest. "We have to talk."

"We will." Bastian kissed her softly again. The reasons lining up in her mind fragmented and melted in desire. He lifted his mouth a fraction from hers. "But can we do it tomorrow?"

"We could."

Tomorrow...

As she slid her hands up his chest to his nape, tomorrow became the promise she made to herself.

Bastian took full possession of her mouth, and waves of need pulled her under, and all that she felt for him took the lead.

Holding on to the front of his shirt, she backed up to the bed and he went with her.

The back of her legs brushed the mattress as he whipped off his shirt. Layla stopped in the middle of unfastening the side zipper on her dress, mesmerized by hard pecs and rows of abs she had to touch.

He interrupted the skimming of her palms over his chest, stepping back to take off his boots and the rest of his clothes.

Caught up in the sight of perfection, she paused.

Bastian captured her mouth and deftly finished the job she'd left undone. As he slid the straps of the dress from her shoulders, his caresses feathered over her skin.

Laying her back on the bed, he removed her lace bra and low-rise bikinis. As he worshipped all that he'd uncovered with heated kisses, she held on to the back of his head, warring with rising pleasure that was too much yet not enough. Overwhelmed by him and what he selflessly gave, she splintered apart.

A short moment later, his erection sheathed in a condom, Bastian glided into her and paused. As he drew in a shaky breath, he met her gaze. He didn't have to say anything. She understood what she saw in his eyes. It was undefined, but raw and real. It made her heart bump in her chest. It made her feel strong and weak at the same time. It fueled a desire so strong for him it almost scared her. It obliterated reason, blocking out the uncertainty ahead. Narrowing her focus to one thing.

Him.

The next morning, Layla woke up in bed in her guest room at Tillbridge, resting on her side under the bedcovers. As she stretched out her legs, Bastian kissed the top of her bare shoulder. Hours earlier, in the middle of the night, that's how round two of their lovemaking had started. She scooted back, expecting to spoon against him, but he wasn't there. Opening her eyes, she rolled to her back.

The light from the corner bathroom illuminated him, laying on his side on top of the comforter without a shirt. His head was on his hand, propped up by his elbow.

Aside from just looking at him, what he had in his hand made her mouth water.

Coffee.

His lips curved up with a slow smile. "Good morning." He held out the cup. "Want some?"

"Yes." Holding the sheet to her chest, she sat up.

He handed her the cup and sat up, too, resting on a pillow against the headboard.

She took a nice long sip of the lightly sweetened brew and sighed. "Thank you."

"You're welcome."

Her eyes adjusted fully to the light, and she took him in. Bastian had on a pair of black sweatpants, and he'd shaved. The scents of soap and his spicy fragrance hovered in the air along with the scent of coffee. "Am I dreaming this?"

Bastian laughed. "You're not dreaming. I'm right here."

The firmness of his lips, and the warmth of his chest as she laid her palm against him, it brought it all back.

She leaned away. "How long have you been up?"

"A couple of hours."

"Wow. I didn't hear you moving around."

"You were out cold. You didn't even hear me when I went out to my truck for my emergency bag."

That explained why he had on sweatpants, instead of the dark jeans he'd had on last night, and his clean-shaven face.

He took hold of her hand and threaded his fingers with hers. "The same thing happened with me when you slipped out of the motel. I didn't wake up because I was that comfortable with you."

She felt the same way with him now. Like they'd

been waking up like this since they'd met and hadn't missed a day together.

But the situation had changed, and there were things she really had to get straight with him before they continued forward. Hopefully, they could move forward.

A chill of anxiety and Bastian gently shaking their joined hands brought Layla from her thoughts. "I can practically hear your mind turning something over. What's wrong?" He tugged her toward him.

She had to put on clothes to talk to him.

Layla spotted her oversize pink sleepshirt bunched near the foot of the bed. She'd put it on last night but had ended up taking it off when she and Bastian had gone in for round two.

"Hold this. I'll be right back." Layla handed him the coffee, snagged the shirt and got out of bed.

In the bathroom, she took care of the essentials. After brushing her teeth and smoothing her hair into a ponytail, she stared at herself in the mirror. He had to trust her and give her time. He just had to take that leap of faith that she was about to ask him to do.

In her mind, she skipped ahead to the day when she didn't have to hold back the truth.

She envisioned telling Bastian everything from who she was to her promise to Grandma Ruby to the offer of the money. He would understand and be on her side. They would talk to Charlotte together, and it would all work out.

That was the best-case scenario. That's what she

hoped for when the time came. But she had to take this first step now to get there.

She walked back into the room.

Bastian still sat on the bed. He was looking at his phone. "I just got a text from Mace. Dominic and Philippa are cooking breakfast for the date night group at Pasture Lane before it opens. We're invited."

How did they know she and Bastian were even together? Did the small-town gossip train travel that fast?

Bastian looked at her. "Do you want to join them? Or do we order room service? I'm good either way."

Enjoying breakfast cooked by a celebrity chef and a group of fun people sounded great. But they should talk.

"Room service might be better."

"I agree. Let's just spend the morning together."

It was seven. They didn't have to be anywhere until ten. That was enough time for her to state her ask from him. A blind leap of faith. That's what embracing complicated required. Would he agree?

He replied to the text and then another chimed in.

"Mace says there's a plan two. Since we can't go to breakfast, can we meet up with everyone at the bar in the Montecito later on today. It's a steak restaurant on the edge of town. The bar also has pool tables, dartboards. It's a decent place. A live band is playing there tonight."

That sounded equally as good as going to breakfast. Especially the dancing part. Did he like to dance? She would have loved doing that with him.

Disappointment lodged in her throat. "Can we take a rain check on that one, too?"

"Sure." Bastian responded then set his phone on the nightstand. He held out his hand. "Now will you come over here and tell me what's on your mind?"

A mix of desire and sincerity drew her to Bastian.

Layla took a breath. Okay, this was it. She sat on the side of the bed next to him.

Another text buzzed on his phone.

The frown on Bastian's face as he glanced at it snagged her attention. "Who is it?"

"It's Gran." He picked up the phone and peered at the text. "She wants me to come by the house this morning at eight for a business meeting."

"A business meeting? Why?"

"I have no idea." He looked up. "She wants you there, too."

Chapter Twenty

Layla parked her rental next to Bastian's truck in front of the garage at Charlotte's house. They had to arrive in separate cars. After the meeting, he was going to Buttons & Lace.

Bastian waited for her near the front of the car. As they walked the path to the house, she pushed her purse strap higher on her shoulder. "You honestly don't know what this is about?"

"Nope. She's never done anything like this before." As they got closer to the porch steps, he took her hand.

"What are we going to tell her about us?"

Bastian intertwined their fingers. "Trust me. She already knows. And it's not a problem."

It might be later on if Charlotte viewed the situation a different way. That her grandson was dating the granddaughter of her enemy.

She walked inside first.

The savory smell of bacon wafted throughout the house.

Bastian arched a brow as he shut the door. "She didn't mention breakfast."

Layla dropped off her purse on the couch, then they walked into the kitchen.

Charlotte arranged place settings at the table. She glanced over at them. "Perfect timing."

Bastian walked over to greet her. "It smells good in here, Gran."

"Thank you." Charlotte paused for him to give her a hug. "I hope you like pancakes, Layla."

"I do. Can I help?"

"The food's warming in the oven. Help me bring it to the table. Sebastian, bring that coffee carafe on the counter. And get the juice out of the fridge, please."

A short time later, fluffy blueberry pancakes, bacon, scrambled eggs, and warm, buttered maple syrup were on the table. Once the juice was poured and everyone had full coffee mugs, they all sat down.

Charlotte encouraged them to fill their plates. "Go on. Eat before it gets cold."

Layla touched Bastian's arm. "Pass the bacon, please?" She accepted the small platter and gave him the bowl of eggs.

As he spooned the eggs on his plate, he glanced at Charlotte's empty one. "Gran, do you want eggs?"

"Not yet." She fiddled with her coffee cup but didn't take a sip.

Layla took a bite of pancakes. Coated with rich syrup, it practically melted in her mouth.

As they took a few more bites, Layla caught Bastian's gaze, wondering what was about to happen.

As if reading her mind, he offered up a subtle shrug.

A short time later, Charlotte interlaced her fingers on top of the table. "I have two things I need to talk about. First, I'm going back to work at the store tomorrow."

Caught with a mouthful of food, Bastian couldn't object, but his expression conveyed what he thought about the idea.

Layla jumped in. "But I thought the doctor had recommended you stay home a bit longer."

"I already talked to her about it."

Bastian took a sip of juice then set down his glass. "When?"

"Last night. While you two were at the Starlight Tasting, I invited Dr. Kyle over for dinner. She examined my knee afterward and gave me the okay to return to work. No heavy lifting and I'm supposed to use the crutch if I'm walking long distances."

"But you don't have to go back now," Bastian said. "Layla, Darby and I have it handled. Why rush back?"

"I know you have it handled, and I appreciate it, but I need to go back for myself. Buttons & Lace is my store, and I can't just lounge around while everyone else does the work. Especially since all three of you are doubled up on jobs. Darby is working at the café and the store. Layla is working shifts and making Eden's dress. You're working shifts and handling repairs here and at the store. You're worried about me overdoing it. What about the three of you? And Bastian, you need to get ready for your job interview."

He shook his head. "You're still recovering from an injury. The three of us aren't. If I have a vote about this, it's no."

"We're not voting, but I'm willing to listen to opinions." Charlotte looked to Layla. "What do you think?"

Layla looked between Charlotte and Bastian, unsure if she should weigh in. Their similarities were at the surface. They both gave off the same level of obstinacy. But she could understand Charlotte's need to return to Buttons & Lace.

Years ago, after Grandma Ruby's car accident, when she was finally back on her feet, she didn't want to sit still either. Everyone had worried about her overdoing it. But she'd needed to fully reengage with life.

Just yesterday, Charlotte had said she'd felt useless. Part of the pact they'd made was for her not to see herself that way. Maybe her decision to return to work now was her way of sticking to it.

Layla chose her words carefully. "If Dr. Kyle has cleared it, I think you should go back to work." Layla shifted her attention to Bastian. "And she won't be entirely on her own. I'll be around and so will you and Darby. And in a few weeks, the new sales associate you hired will have started."

Bastian held her gaze for a beat longer before looking to Charlotte.

He released a long exhale. "I'll support you if you're going to follow Dr. Kyle's instructions. And maybe you should consider keeping the abbreviated store hours in place a little while longer."

Charlotte smiled. "That's fair."

Bastian moved his plate away. "What's the other thing you wanted to talk about?"

"You." Charlotte squared her shoulders. "As your boss, I'm mandating that you take time off from the shop before your interview. You need to be relaxed and rested for it."

A chuckle shot out of him. "My boss?"

"Yes, I'm pulling rank." She gave him a serene smile. "Following the chain of command is something you understand."

"I do." He gave her a mock solute. "Yes, ma'am."

As they exchanged smiles, their affection for each other clearly showed in their eyes.

"It's settled then." Charlotte put a pancake on her plate.

After breakfast, as Bastian got ready to leave for the shop, he took Layla's hand, and she went with him to the front door.

"Thank you for helping me see things the right way with my gran."

"You're welcome." As he glided his palms around her waist, she linked her hands at his nape.

He widened his stance and brought her closer. "I don't want to go anywhere. I wish I could just spend the day with you."

"I do, too."

"Call or text me about meeting up with everyone at the Montecito. Or do you still want to talk? Sorry, I didn't mean to forget about that. I can come by Tillbridge or you can meet me here at the guest cottage. That's where I'm sleeping these days."

Talking. They needed to do that. Bastian made it so easy not to focus on priorities. "We should talk. Can I call or text you later and let you know where?"

"Sure."

Bastian pressed his lips to hers, and Layla thought of their "last kiss" in the driveway. The kiss they were sharing then might actually be one of their last ones if Bastian decided her level of complicated was too much.

It was almost too much for her. Before arriving in Bolan, there had only been one difficult conversation she'd needed to have. Now there were two.

In the kitchen, Charlotte glanced up from where she loaded plates into the dishwasher. "Thank you for being here this morning. And for helping me convince Bastian that I should go back to work."

"You're welcome. I could tell it was important to you." Layla didn't feel like smiling but she forced one for Charlotte. She went to the table to gather up the serving platters and bowls.

"It is important to me to get back to running my business. But I also have to go back for Bastian."

Layla paused to look at her. "I don't understand."

Charlotte came to the table and sat down. She gestured for Layla to do the same. "The interview that's coming up for him, he really wants the position. And he might have already been hired if I hadn't gotten hurt. Now all he's doing is worrying about me and the store. I don't want him carrying those worries with him into the interview, or worse, he decides not to take the job because he thinks he has to look after me. I need him to know that I'm fine. I would feel terrible if he lost this opportunity because of me."

Wanting the best for their grandchildren. Grandma Ruby and Charlotte were alike in that respect. It was sad that they didn't know this about each other. That they had differences but also wonderful similarities.

Layla laid her hand on Charlotte's. "I'm sure he'll do well."

"You're right. He will." Charlotte dabbed away coming tears with her fingers. "He's taking time off like I asked him. And he has you. I'm so glad you're back together. And that you two are spending time with his friends. He's happy. Being with you is a good distraction. You're exactly what he needs."

Layla wasn't sure how to respond. Would Charlotte say the same when she found out who she was?

Later that evening, Layla walked to her car in the driveway. She was meeting Bastian at the cottage in a couple of hours for their talk. And she wasn't looking forward to it.

Bastian's truck pulled into the driveway. He parked beside her and got out.

As he strode over to her, a big smile was on his face.

Before she could say anything, he took her in his arms and kissed her.

Her world spun. Her heart felt heavy with dread and swelled with desire for him at the same time.

He lifted his mouth from hers. "Hi."

"Hey." She caught her breath. "Why are you home so early?"

"I couldn't wait to see you." He pecked a kiss on her nose. "And it was slow." He pecked another kiss on her lips. "I was able to get a lot of stuff done early so I could leave right at five. Or maybe it was five minutes earlier than that." He laughed then pressed a lingering kiss on her lips. "I thought about you all day, but you were a good distraction."

A good distraction. That's what Charlotte had said she was for him.

Layla looked up at Bastian. Their talk could take him from being in a happy place to one that disrupted his focus.

Talking to him was important. He had to have the opportunity to decide if he still wanted to pursue a relationship with her under the terms she had to lay out. But did that have to happen now? Or could it wait a few more days until after he'd nailed his interview?

They both shifted their stance and slightly swayed as they held each other.

He laid his forehead to hers. "What are you thinking?"

"Let's go dancing tonight."

Chapter Twenty-One

"Do you work better independently or as part of a team?" As Layla asked Bastian the question, she wore a professional game face.

But sitting next to her on the porch swing at the cottage, all he could think about was kissing her.

"That depends." He stretched his arm behind her. "Are you on my team?"

As he leaned in, Layla held up the paper, blocking the kiss. "A bad pickup line, that's definitely the wrong answer."

"Bad pickup line?" A chuckle shot out of him. "Ouch."

She nudged him back. "Stop playing around and stick to the program. Next question—"

"I've answered every question on that list at least four times."

"Five times the charm."

He slipped the paper from her hand and set it next to him. "I can practically recite the answers in my sleep."

"The interview is tomorrow. I just want you to feel ready."

"The panel interview is the day after tomorrow, and I am ready—thanks to you." Caring filled her eyes. Taking advantage of her silence, he went in for the kiss he'd been longing for.

Seven days ago, after their breakfast with Gran, she'd checked in with him about the interview. The confession about not having done one in a while had just slipped out.

The next day, she'd come to him with a list of interview Q and A's she'd found online. They were similar to the ones he already reviewed, but she'd been so enthusiastic about helping him, he couldn't say no. And it had given them another reason to spend time together. He just hadn't counted on her turning into a drill sergeant...but her ordering him to focus and stay on task was sexy, too.

Layla eased away from him. "I should go. Charlotte's waiting for me."

"I thought you two were at a standstill with the wedding dress?"

"Unfortunately, yes."

"What happened? Gran didn't tell me."

"There was a mix-up with one of our lace orders.

A glitch happened when they processed the payment. They never called us, and the lace was sold to someone else."

"That's the second time a glitch has happened with the store's credit card. What did Gran say about it?"

"Stop." She laid her hand on his leg. "You're worrying about Buttons & Lace when you should be concentrating on your interview. Charlotte is checking on the card, and I already took care of the lace issue. I called Kinsley. She was able to tap into one of her contacts. Fingers crossed, the lace should be here in a few days. In the meantime, Charlotte and I have a bridesmaid dress emergency to take care of. And you should finish packing."

"Yeah, I should." He was making the two-and-a-half-hour drive to Alexandria that night.

A tour of MaxPointe's facilities with Aaron was on tomorrow morning's agenda. The next day he'd go through the interview, and the day after attend a couple of shake-and-grins with key staff so they could size him up.

Three days. Now that he and Layla were back together, it felt like a really long time to be away from her.

As she stood, Bastian took hold of her hand.

She looked back at him and smiled. "What?"

Thoughts about her, about them staying together for the long term, which he hadn't quite processed yet, sifted through his mind. And there was no reason to mention them, at least not until he'd sorted out his job situation.

"Are you good with all the security codes for here?"

While he was gone, Layla was staying at the cottage. From there, she could easily put in more time on the dress when the lace arrived and keep an eye on his grandmother.

"Yes. I put everything on my phone and the key to this house and Charlotte's is on my key ring."

"Good." He gave her hand a quick squeeze. "I'll be up at the house in about half an hour."

"Okay. I'll tell Charlotte."

Layla walked across the grass, heading back to the house. Her stride was graceful and easy as if she was comfortable in herself and the space around her. She looked really happy.

"I'm in between places in my life right now. I'm... taking time to figure out what I want."

That's what Layla had said three weeks ago. But what if she'd found what she wanted in Bolan? What if the two of them being together was the right place in her life. And right for him, too?

Layla stood in front of the mirror in Charlotte's workroom, wearing the blue bridesmaid's dress and heels. Cut from chiffon, the floor-length creation had a V neckline, fitted bodice and a cascading ruffle starting from the side hip of the skirt and opening into a slit.

Charlotte sat on the floor, checking the hem.

The bridesmaid who would wear the dress worked for a relief organization and was somewhere remote. And there was a possibility she wouldn't arrive until the night before the wedding.

Another seamstress had shortened the dress and delivered it to Poppy and Eden for safekeeping. But Poppy hadn't liked the work that had been done and had asked Charlotte to redo it.

Since Layla was approximately the same height as the bridesmaid, she was standing in.

Charlotte tsked. "The hem is uneven, and the dress is too short. And there's not enough fabric to make the adjustment. If Poppy would have bought the bridesmaids' dresses from me in the first place, this wouldn't have happened."

Layla helped Charlotte up. Her knee was a lot better, but it was still a little tender. "What are you going to do?"

"The only thing I can do at this point. Deliver the bad news to Poppy." Charlotte left to find her phone.

Layla checked out the dress in the mirror. Aside from the hem being slanted, the dress was pretty. It had an underskirt that added gentle movement. And the side slit was perfect for dancing.

Layla moved her hips to a beat she made up in her head. As she spun around, she ran into Bastian's gaze.

"Hey." Slightly embarrassed, she laughed.

He ambled into the room. "That's beautiful."

"It really is." Layla glanced down at the dress. "Eden made a good pick."

"No." Bastian wrapped an arm around her waist. With his other hand, he took hold of hers and flattened it to his chest. "*You* look beautiful moving in that dress. You're beautiful."

"Thank you." Following his lead, she swayed with him in a slow dance.

A week ago, they had gone to the bar at the Montecito to join the date-night group. They'd had fun eating bar food, playing pool and darts. And dancing.

Unlike the night of the Starlight Tasting, they were able to embrace being a couple. They'd snuck in so many kisses, the group had teased them and told them to get a room.

Laying her head to his chest, she breathed him in and listened to his steady heartbeat. She wished time could stand still. That this dance could last forever.

Minutes later, his chest rose and fell with a long breath. "I have to go."

She lifted her head and looked up at him. "I know."

He kissed the back of her hand. "Thanks for the dance."

"You're welcome." She met him halfway for a gentle kiss on the lips.

When it ended, Bastian caressed her cheek. For a fleeting moment, a pensive expression came over his face. A small smile tipped up his mouth. Kissing her on the forehead, he released her slowly from his embrace and walked out the door.

Standing in the middle of the room, she already felt lonely without him.

Charlotte came back in. "I spoke to Poppy. She

thinks we might be able to swap this dress with one from a bridesmaid who's shorter. Apparently, her dress is too long."

The engine to Bastian's truck reverberated.

As the sound of the truck grew more distant, unexplained tears sprang up in Layla's eyes.

Charlotte inspected a side seam in the bodice. "This doesn't look right either. Does this side of the dress feel tighter when you move around in it?"

"Maybe." Blinking back tears, Layla sniffed.

"Are you okay?"

"Uh-huh. I just got the sniffles all of a sudden."

Charlotte met Layla's gaze in the mirror. Compassion came into her eyes. "Is it allergies?"

"Yes, that's probably it." Even as Layla laughed at their inside joke, tears escaped from her eyes. She swiped at her cheeks. "I have no idea why I'm weepy all of a sudden."

"Don't you?" Charlotte wrapped an arm around her waist. "You're falling for him."

Layla's tears started to dry up. Was she? "No. We just met. It's too soon for that."

"If you truly care about him, it's never too soon. Come here for a minute." Charlotte led her over to the bench seat under the window and they sat down.

She kept holding Layla's hand. "Before my daughter's father, there was someone. His name was Richard, and he was in the navy. A buddy of his lived in the next town and he was visiting him. They used to come to Bolan for ice cream. His buddy was cute, but Richard." She fanned her face. "Talk about tall, dark and handsome. I couldn't believe he wanted to talk to me."

"Why not? You're beautiful."

"Thank you." Charlotte smiled. "But at twenty-one, I may have had the looks, but what I needed was courage. Richard and I spent two weeks together. When I saw him off at the airport in D.C., I wanted to tell him so badly how I felt about him, but I didn't. I can't speak for Richard, but I wish I would have had the courage to be truthful with myself and him. If I had, I would know the outcome. But instead all I can do is wonder what might have been if he'd known how much I'd cared about him."

Prompted by what Charlotte had just said, Layla shared what was in her heart. "It's happened so fast with Bastian and I. It scares me a little. What if he doesn't feel the same way I do?"

"What?" Charlotte scoffed. "Have you seen his face when he looks at you? But you're not alone in being scared. He is, too."

"How do you know?"

Charlotte looked down at their hands and took a breath. "I love my daughter with every fiber of my being, but I can't deny that her choices weren't always the best ones. Growing up, everything bored her, especially this town. She had Sebastian when she was sixteen. As soon as she turned eighteen, she packed a bag and took him with her." Charlotte's face grew sad with a faraway look. "She dragged him from place to place. And when things got tough, she would drop him here. I always gave her money to get back on her feet. Weeks or months later, she'd show up and take him away again."

Layla couldn't imagine what Bastian had faced. The one thing her father had worked hard to give her and Tyler after their mom died was a stable home.

"That must have been so chaotic for him."

"It was. She basically taught him not to hold on to things or people too tightly. When he was fifteen, she met someone. He had money but he didn't want children. She told Sebastian he couldn't be with them because her job required too much travel. He found out it wasn't true. She just didn't need him to get money from me anymore."

"She just abandoned him?"

Charlotte nodded. "And she broke his heart. I did my best to show him that it's okay to care for someone. And I'd honestly thought I'd failed. But then he met you. He let you in."

Hearing about Bastian's past raised so many emotions in Layla. As well as deep respect for him and for how Charlotte had managed to raise him into the man he was today. He was dependable, honorable, strong. He'd let her into his life. And she so desperately wanted to let him into hers, but...

"I don't know what to do." The whispered words, that were more for herself, slipped out of Layla.

Charlotte turned more toward Layla and held her hand in both of hers. "Tell Bastian how you feel. I'm so afraid that he won't. I don't want you two to miss out on a future you could have together. I probably shouldn't say this, but I will. I want him to have a home and a stable life with someone with all that he deserves from this world. And I'm hoping that someone is you."

"Oh, Charlotte…" Mixed emotions of fear and feeling touched by Charlotte's hopes clogged Layla's throat. Like Bastian, there was so much Charlotte didn't know.

"It's okay." She patted Layla's hand. "You don't have to say anything. And I know I've probably said too much too soon. But, if I could ask for one thing, just promise me that you'll tell him how you feel."

As Layla looked into Charlotte's eyes, the truth about who she was almost tumbled out. No. She had to tell Bastian everything first, including the truth about how she felt about him. And why she'd held back on telling him until now.

Layla nodded. "I will."

Later that night, Layla lay in bed at the guest cottage, but she couldn't sleep. The faint woodsy scent emanating from Bastian's pillows made her ache with longing. And every possible scenario of what could happen once he got home, along with what Charlotte had told her earlier, kept playing through her mind.

Her phone buzzed on the nightstand.

A text from Bastian lit up the screen.

Miss you.

She answered.

Miss you, too.

Dots floated in a message, disappeared and came back again.

Why aren't you asleep?

Because I have a secret that I just can't hold on to anymore—actually, two of them. I'm falling in love with you and I'm Ruby Morris's granddaughter. And I'm really hoping that my first secret will cancel out the other and that we can stay together and find out if what we have is a temporary thing or something more. I really want it to be more...
But she couldn't say any of that. Not yet.
Layla tapped in a response.

I will now that I've heard from you. I'm hugging your pillow and pretending it's you.

A short moment later, a new message bubble appeared.

Lucky pillow. You won't have to pretend for long. I'll be home soon. Sweet dreams.

Chapter Twenty-Two

One more day...

Layla let the reminder seep into her thoughts as she hung up blouses on a rack at Buttons & Lace. That's how long she had until Bastian came home. And then she could straighten everything out. Or at least she hoped she could.

Grandma Ruby had phoned while she was driving with Charlotte to the store. She was probably as impatient as Tyler by now. But before she spoke to her, she wanted to talk to Bastian and Charlotte.

And that would happen soon.

The lace for Eden's dress was arriving by special delivery that afternoon. Once she sewed the remainder of the design on the train, the dress would be done. And she could free herself of all the secrets she'd held on to since arriving in Bolan.

Apprehension and relief tightened in her belly. Think positive. That's what she needed to do right now. And believe in what Bastian always told her. Together, they would figure it out.

"Darn it!" Charlotte swiped a duster along the wall near the ceiling. "There's a cobweb in the corner and I can't reach it."

As she went to climb on the stepladder, Layla hurried over to her. What was up with Charlotte? She'd been snippy since she'd come out of the office a few minutes ago, and they hadn't even opened the store yet.

"I'll get it." Layla slipped the duster from her grasp.

"I'm not useless, remember?" Charlotte's cheeks were a light shade of pink that almost matched her shirt. "And why didn't one of you see it in the first place? It was there plain as day."

The accusation and snap in her voice made Layla pause.

An apologetic look crept over Charlotte's face. She closed her eyes for a moment. "I'm sorry. I didn't mean that. You, Bastian and Darby have done a great job of keeping up with the store."

Layla extended the pole. Rising on the toes of her black flats, she snagged the tiny web she hadn't noticed earlier.

From the few specks of dust falling on her pale

blue blouse and navy slacks, the molding near the ceiling probably could use a good dusting.

She would do it. And she would also convince Charlotte to go home after lunch. She looked tired. "Are you okay?"

"Yes." Charlotte ran her palms down the front of her beige skirt. "I'm just a little frustrated. I can't find the invoice for the shoe order. I probably left it at the house."

"I think that one is in your emails. They've switched to paperless billing. Bastian said he was going to talk to you about it."

"Paperless." Charlotte huffed a breath. "That's what everyone's doing. I like a hard copy for my files."

"I can pull up the email and print it."

"Would you? I want to rearrange the purse display before we open."

"No problem."

Layla went into the office.

She couldn't stop her gaze from drifting to the wedding dress draped on the mannequin.

The bodice with a princess neckline had a delicate overlay of lace that matched the long off-the-shoulder sleeves that Eden had coveted. The slightly billowing skirt had a detachable, chapel-length train that, once it was finished, would feature an intricate floral design.

Excitement, pride, even a tiny bit of awe that the dress was real, hit Layla just like it had over the past few days whenever she saw it. Had *she* done this? Perhaps her pact with Charlotte had worked. And maybe just like her mom and Grandma Ruby, she had weaved a little magic into the dress.

Layla walked to the desk and focused on the task at hand.

Maybe she should create a folder on the desktop for the electronic invoices. If she showed Charlotte how to upload them to one spot, she might appreciate the convenience of going paperless.

As she tapped the mouse to open the email app, a spreadsheet appeared on the screen—last quarter's balance sheet for Buttons & Lace. The totals near the bottom grabbed her attention. Liabilities exceeded assets by an amount that made her look twice. That couldn't be right. Surely, it was an error. She clicked around the spreadsheet checking the numbers. All of the formulas supporting the spreadsheet were correct. Layla opened the last two quarters and saw the same outcomes.

Charlotte strode into the office. "Layla, did all of the purses from the last order come in?" She met Layla's gaze and wariness shadowed her face. "Did you find the email?"

"No. I was just about to look for it."

"I'll do it." Charlotte hurried over to the desk and nudged her out of the way. She fumbled with the computer mouse, trying to close the spreadsheet. "Why are you snooping around?"

"I wasn't snooping. The app was open." Concern

prompted Layla to ask. "Charlotte, are those numbers right?"

"That's none of your business."

"Does Bastian know?"

"It's under control."

How many times had a client told her that—only to lose everything because they wouldn't listen. "Charlotte, you're in serious debt."

"I'm handling it. I've already made arrangements for a loan with a company. I'm signing the papers later today."

A company and not a bank? "How will you pay it back? The store's not making nearly enough to get you out of this…" The answer dawned clearly in Layla's mind. Charlotte had one solid asset. "You're using your home as collateral. No, that's a mistake."

"I have to…" As Charlotte pressed her lips together, her eyes grew bright with unshed tears. "I don't have a choice. And I'm not bothering Bastian about it. He's already done too much for me. Like I told you, he needs to focus on his future."

"But taking out the loan is not right, Charlotte. Let's find another way."

"No." Charlotte shook her head. "This is how I want to handle it, and you're staying out of it."

But she couldn't stay out of it. She couldn't let Charlotte lose her home. Layla stood in front of her. "I'll give you the money."

"I won't take it."

As Charlotte sidestepped around her to walk out of the office, Layla saw the solution clearly in her mind.

The realization filled Layla with sadness. It squeezed around her heart so fiercely, she closed her eyes. She opened them again and saw Charlotte near the threshold.

It hurt so much to say it, Layla had to push out the words. "You'll take the money. If you don't, I'll tell Bastian."

Charlotte faced her. "You wouldn't."

"I would."

As Charlotte walked back into the office, the devastation was in her eyes. "Don't do this."

Layla almost choked on her response. "I have to."

Grandma Ruby's curse would be lifted. Tyler would get her fashion debut. Charlotte would keep her home. Eden would get her dress. And Bastian would be free to pursue his career.

But this bargain. This final secret between her and Charlotte wouldn't allow her to have a relationship with Bastian. She had to leave. And like a cruel joke, she didn't even have to reveal who she was.

As Charlotte stared back at her, Layla saw the depth of the hurt she was causing, and she also caught a glimpse of what might have occurred forty years ago when Ruby and Charlotte had their disagreement.

Just like now, Charlotte most likely not only felt hurt. She'd believed Ruby, her friend and business partner, had betrayed her.

Charlotte lifted her head and squared her shoulders. The kindness that had once reflected in her eyes toward Layla was gone.

A queasy sensation roiled inside of Layla. If only Charlotte could see she wasn't her enemy but someone who truly cared about her welfare.

The back door opened.

They both recognized the booted footfalls.

Charlotte's gaze met Layla's. She nodded. The look of resignation in her eyes also gave her answer. She would accept the money.

Bastian strode into the office. "Hey, I'm home." Looking between Charlotte and Layla, he frowned. "What's wrong?"

"Nothing." Charlotte reanimated. "You just surprised us." Smiling, she hugged him. "You're home. I thought you weren't coming back until tomorrow?"

"I was in a hurry to get back." As Charlotte released him, he glanced at Layla. "And there really wasn't a reason to stay. They already offered me the job."

"They did?" Charlotte clasped her hands together. "That's wonderful. Isn't it, Layla?"

Torn between happiness for Bastian and her own unhappiness, Layla forced a smile. "Yes, that's really wonderful."

A loud knock sounded on the front door.

"Someone's anxious to start shopping." Charlotte laughed. "I'll open up. Layla, we'll talk about that paperwork issue later. Can you shut down the computer for me?" She kissed Bastian on the cheek and hurried up front.

As Bastian went to Layla, he pointed his thumb over his shoulder. "Is she okay? She's opening fifteen minutes early."

"She probably doesn't want to lose a potential sale." Layla closed the spreadsheet.

Bastian joined her behind the desk and took hold of her waist. He smiled. "Hey, do I get a kiss?"

Layla turned to him. The sadness free-floating inside of her welled into a bittersweetness that tightened in her throat. Resting her palms on his chest, she resisted the urge to hold on to him. If she did, she might not let go. This was their last kiss. But before it happened, she needed him to know just how much she cared about him.

"Bastian, I—"

"No!" Charlotte's cry reverberated down the hallway.

Bastian let go of Layla and flew out of the office.

Alarm surging through her, Layla ran behind him to the front of the store.

Charlotte lay on the ground near the entrance. A dark-haired woman with her back toward them knelt beside her.

Bastian kept running, but recognition froze Layla in place.

"Gran?" Bastian dropped down next to Charlotte and took her hand. "Gran, can you hear me?"

Her eyes fluttered opened. "Ruby Morris—but it

can't be you. You look younger than you did forty years ago. Are you dead?"

"Dead?" The woman reared back slightly. "She's not dead."

"Who are you?" Bastian asked.

Layla met Tyler's gaze. "She's my sister. Ruby Morris is our grandmother."

Chapter Twenty-Three

Bastian paced in front of a row of black chairs in the half-empty waiting area of the hospital emergency room.

During the ambulance ride, Charlotte had started experiencing chest pains.

This couldn't be happening. He couldn't lose her. What was going on? Why hadn't the doctor come out to see him yet?

Mace nodded in agreement to something a nurse at the station said to him. He'd been on duty and heard the 911 call for the ambulance.

He walked over to Bastian. "They're still evaluating Charlotte. Dr. Kyle is already here at the hospital. She was checking on a patient. She's on her way down."

A small bit of relief flooded through Bastian. "That's good to know. Hopefully, she'll give me an update." The image of his gran in the ambulance, wearing an oxygen mask, played through his mind. Shutting his eyes, he scrubbed a hand over his face.

Mace gripped him by the shoulder. "Hang in there. Your grandmother is tough. Have faith." His gaze moved past Bastian's shoulder to the side hallway. "Good. Layla's here."

Layla... Was it true? Was she Ruby Morris's granddaughter? Confusion swam in the anxiety pooled inside of him. A part of him wanted to know what was going on. Another part of him didn't.

She came to him, worry filling her face. "We got here as fast as we could. How's Charlotte?"

We?

The woman named Tyler stood a few feet away.

That's right. Layla had a sister.

Mace looked at the three of them. From his expression, he sensed something was up. "We're still waiting on word about how she is. Dr. Kyle is here. She's going to help evaluate her."

"That's good." Layla laid a hand on Bastian's arm. "Do you need anything?"

Need anything? He needed to understand what was going on. "We should talk outside."

Mace met his gaze and nodded. "I'll come get you if something changes."

Outside the double sliding doors of the emergency room, Bastian walked a few feet down the sidewalk with Layla.

Frustration did a slow burn inside of him. He stopped to face her. "Tell me what happened this morning. No, start by telling me what's been going on since you've been here."

Layla visibly swallowed. "I came to Bolan to talk to Charlotte on behalf of my grandmother."

"Talk? You've been here for three weeks, and you never mentioned her name or why you came here."

"I'd planned to tell you and Charlotte." She reached out to him. "I really wanted to, but I couldn't."

I wanted to... I couldn't...

Her words scored him like a dull blade. They were straight from his mother's playbook. All Layla would give him was a meaningless explanation that couldn't excuse the inexcusable.

Mace motioned to him from the door.

"I need to go back inside."

"Please." Layla grasped his arm. "I never meant to hurt you. What can I do?" The emotional pain on her face looked real, but how could he tell? Did he ever really know her at all?

He didn't have the time or the extra energy to figure it out. His gran needed him. "I can't do this right now. Just go."

As Bastian walked back inside, anguish took Layla's breath away. She wanted to be there for him. For Charlotte. She'd never forgive herself if something happened to her.

Tyler joined her outside.

During the fifteen-mile rush to the hospital, they hadn't talked.

She met Layla on the sidewalk. "He looks really upset. Is everything okay?"

"Of course he's upset." Layla's tone rose with her despair and frustration. "His grandmother is in the hospital." She dropped her head in her hands for a moment, trying to gain some composure. "What are you doing here?"

"I came to see you."

"How did you even know where to find me?"

"I was at your office when Kinsley's assistant called to confirm the Maryland address for your lace order. When Naomi told her the address, I wrote it down."

"And after that, you just hopped on a plane?"

"What else was I supposed to do? You wouldn't tell me what was going on."

Layla drew in a breath, ready to lash out at Tyler. But what would that solve? It wouldn't erase what happened. Closing her eyes, she released a slow exhale. If she'd learned anything from the situation between Grandma Ruby and Charlotte, it was how easily a disagreement could drive a wedge between two people. No matter how much they cared about each other.

Her phone rang with a familiar ringtone. Grandma Ruby's. She'd forgotten to phone her back.

Maybe this call was a sign. No, the sign was Charlotte being in the hospital. Tears stung in Layla's eyes. There wasn't any point in keeping things hidden any longer.

She answered. "Hi, Grandma."

"I've been trying to reach you. Patrice told me Tyler went to Maryland. She isn't with you, is she?"

As Layla spoke on the phone, she looked to Tyler. "Yes, she's here. We're at the hospital."

"The hospital?" Concern filled Ruby's voice. "What happened? Are you hurt? Is Tyler okay?"

"We're fine." Layla took a shaky breath as sorrow filled her chest. "It's Charlotte. She collapsed this morning and had to be taken to the emergency room."

"Oh no...that's terrible."

"My plan... It didn't work. I failed. I thought I could help but I've made a mess of everything. And now Charlotte..." Layla feared the worst.

Grandma Ruby remained silent for moment. She released a deep sigh. "No, you didn't make a mess of anything. I did. Put Tyler on."

"She wants to talk to you." After handing Tyler the phone, Layla sat on a bench at the edge of the sidewalk.

"Hi, Grandma." For several minutes, Tyler just listened. Her brow rose as she looked to Layla. "Oh. I...okay. I will. I love you, too."

After ending the call, Tyler dropped down beside her. "Seriously? A curse?" She shook her head. "I don't understand. Grandma was never overly superstitious. And why did you go along with it?"

"I didn't go along with it exactly." Drained of the

secret she'd held on to for weeks, Layla felt as if so much more of her had been lost along with it. "Honestly, in my opinion, superstition had nothing to do with what happened. Charlotte and Grandma were like sisters. I think their fight just left a lot of things unresolved—for both of them. It still is."

For a long moment, they stared out at the parking lot. From Tyler's face, she was still digesting the news.

"I've messed things up for you, haven't I? I'm so sorry." She clasped Layla's hand on the bench. "I should have trusted you and stayed out of the way. Would it help if I talked to Charlotte's grandson?"

"No. I'm the one who has to talk to Bastian. We have a lot to work out."

Tyler's eyes widened. "Oh…so you two are together?"

"Just go…" The way Bastian said it had sounded so final. But he probably didn't mean it that way. He was worried, upset about Charlotte. "I don't know… We were."

Sincerity and concern showed on Tyler's face. She squeezed Layla's hand. "Are you sure there isn't anything I can do?"

Turn the clock back for a do-over. But to what point in time? Maybe all the way back to Eden, Poppy and the wedding dresses? *The dress…* The lace was arriving that afternoon.

"You can come with me back to the store." Layla stood. "I have a promise to keep."

Less than an hour later, Layla and Tyler walked in the back door of Buttons & Lace and into the office.

During the drive, Layla had told Tyler about the store, the dress and Bastian.

Layla put the package she'd just signed for on the worktable.

As Tyler set her tote bag beside it, she gaped at the dress. "Oh my gosh, you did this?"

"With Charlotte's guidance." As Layla circled the mannequin along with her, she fluffed the skirt. "But it wasn't completely my inspiration or anything. Eden told me what she wanted, and I pulled it together."

"Pulled it together? You killed it."

A compliment from her fashion phenom sister? That was a first. A sliver of pride broke through the growing gloom and anxiousness Layla had felt since leaving the hospital. "You really think so?"

"Yes." Tyler wrapped an arm around her. "This is beautiful. What do you need me to do to help you finish it?"

"The train…" Layla opened the package. "I still have to finish the pattern. That's why I needed the lace—for the design."

Tyler traced her finger over the lace. "I can see why you chose this. It's so elegant. Why don't I cut the pattern and you pin it?"

"That's perfect."

Soon they were immersed in the process. For Layla it was stop and start as she waited on customers until Darby arrived.

Time passed mostly in silence in the office with Tyler checking in when needed for directions. Once the pattern was pinned to the tulle, with Tyler's help, Layla focused intently on sewing the appliquéd design.

During a quick break, Layla sent a text to Bastian, checking on him and Charlotte. She let him know where she was and asked if he needed anything.

Bastian sent back a brief response.

We're good.

So that meant Charlotte was okay, right? Was she still in the hospital or had she been discharged? Layla debated asking for more details. Bastian had his hands full. The best way she could help was to stay on task.

That evening, shortly after the store closed for business, Layla attached the finished train to the dress.

Tyler smiled. "There is no way in the world Eden or her mother won't love this."

"It's good."

"Good?" Tyler stared at her as if she'd lost it. "This is fabulous."

"Like you wouldn't have done this ten times better and in half the time. Everyone knows you're more talented than me. That's why Grandma took you under her wing."

"She took me under her wing because I was a hellion." Tyler chuckled. "Her words. Not mine. She said she had to keep me busy so I would stay out of trouble. She knew you were fine. Do you know how many times I heard how talented you were, and how I should be more like you?"

"Talented?" Confused, Layla dropped down in the chair at the sewing machine. "But she never told me that."

"Probably because she didn't want to pressure you." Tyler picked up scraps of lace that had fallen to the floor and put them on the table. "I remember how devastated she was when you announced that you were becoming an accountant. She cried for three days after you left for college. We couldn't tell you because she said if we did, there would be greater than hell to pay. We all clammed up because no one wanted a part of that."

"Seriously?"

Tyler mimed locking her mouth shut and tossing the key.

Layla grappled with the revelation. Except for when she'd made the initial announcement, Grandma Ruby had always been enthusiastic about her career choice.

Tyler stared at the wedding dress as she leaned back on the edge of the table. "So all this time, you could have been creating dresses like this and you didn't?"

"Yeah, sort of." She met Tyler's gaze and pointed at her. "Same penalty conditions as Grandma's if you tell this, but when I go to visit Kinsley, I'm not really lounging at her pool. I'm helping her sew prom dresses and evening gowns for her pop-up store."

Tyler's mouth dropped open. "Shut up. What about all those pictures you posted online of you two indulging in spa days, drinking cocktails and eating gourmet food?"

"Staged. Staged. The food…well, that wasn't staged. Kinsley's husband—the man can cook. Once we took a few photos, Kinsley and I went back to work."

"Wow." Tyler threw back her head and laughed. "I was always so envious because I thought you were having such a good time enjoying life."

"I was enjoying life. Making dresses with Kinsley made me happy."

"But didn't getting your fashion fix only once a year feel stifling?"

"Sometimes."

"So why did you keep limiting yourself?"

Telling yourself you're not good enough is what's stopping you from seeing your talent…

Maybe Charlotte was right.

Layla's gaze drifted to Eden's dress. "Because I believed I wasn't good enough. But honestly, I don't know if I could have done this without Charlotte nudging me along."

Please let her be okay… No news could be good news, right?

Tyler took her phone from her bag and snapped photos of the dress. "Well, the myth of you not being good enough is forever shattered. You do realize you can't go back to being an accountant now?"

"Why not?"

Her sister pointed to the wedding gown. "Creating that, and then trying not to create anything like it, is the equivalent of trying to unsee something you already saw. You can't."

A knock sounded at the back door.

Layla's heart bumped in her chest but settled. Bastian had a key. Maybe it was a late delivery? She opened the door.

Mace stood outside. No longer in uniform, he wore casual clothes. "Hi, Layla." His expression remained neutral as he stepped inside.

"Hi. Do you know how Charlotte's doing? I sent Bastian a text earlier, but he didn't say much. Just that they were fine."

"It looks like Charlotte had a severe panic attack. But Dr. Kyle still has a few minor concerns. They're keeping her overnight for observation. Bastian's going to stay at the hospital with her."

Relief trickled through Layla, weakening her knees. "I'm so glad. Did Bastian mention if he needed anything—his truck is here. I guess I should call to see if he wants me to bring it to him."

"That's probably not a good idea." Mace looked directly in her eyes. "He told me to tell you that he would prefer you not be here or at Charlotte's cottage when they come back tomorrow."

The weight of Bastian's request struck hard and deep. Shock ricocheted inside of Layla. She'd thought he'd want to talk to her about the past few weeks. That she'd get a chance to explain. Ask for forgiveness.

"Oh...okay. I'll leave town tonight."

Mace's expression grew empathetic. "I'm sure that's not what he intended. I'll call Zurie. You can stay at Tillbridge tonight."

"No." Bastian had meant what he said. He really did want her to go. "You're his friends. I don't want to come between you. I'll do what he's asking."

Mace released a long breath. "I don't know what happened with you two, but right now, he's twisted up over Charlotte. She's pretty much all the family he has. Once he knows she's okay, I'm sure he'll reach out. Are you sure you don't want to stay at Tillbridge in case he changes his mind?"

Mace's kindness toward her along with sadness made it hard for Layla to speak. "I'm sure. I'll leave my keys to everything at the cottage. Please tell Zurie and everyone goodbye for me."

He studied her a moment then gave a nod. "Will do."

Mace left and Tyler came out of the office. From her concerned expression, she'd heard everything. "He's kicking you out?"

"It's okay."

"It's not okay. I'll go to the hospital and talk to Bastian. This is my fault. I caused Charlotte's panic attack." Tyler turned to get her purse from the office.

"No. This entire situation is my fault. I kept too much from him. He has every right to be upset. And right now, Charlotte needs him." The new reality she'd feared had come true. She'd lost him. "We should clean up. I need to pack."

A few hours later at Charlotte's cottage, they stowed their bags in the back of the rental. Tyler had looked up flights. The best option had been to leave tomorrow from Philadelphia. It was two hours away.

Tyler slipped the car keys out of her hand. "I'm driving."

"Thanks." Layla got in the front passenger seat. It was probably best. Her thoughts were all over the place, but she'd been too numb to cry.

As they passed Charlotte's house, memories of laughing with her in the workroom, sharing meals, creative ideas, and listening to Charlotte's wisdom passed through her mind. She'd come here to give Charlotte something, but Charlotte had given her more. She'd given her confidence. A new appreciation for dressmaking. And because of her, she'd met Bastian. But now she'd lost him.

Misery grew inside of Layla, and her heart squeezed. Tears pricked in her eyes, but they still wouldn't fall.

At the end of the driveway, Tyler turned right instead of left.

Layla pointed behind them. "The fastest route is that way."

"We're not going to Philadelphia yet. We're going to Virginia Beach. I made reservations for us at a spa resort. We're staying there for a few days."

Virginia... Where Bastian had just gotten a job.

Would he still go? It wouldn't be because Charlotte was in debt. She'd make sure of that. "We should get back home."

"No. We shouldn't. You need some time before going back to Atlanta. It's all set up. I'm taking care of you for a change."

What she needed was for Bastian to forgive her, and a second chance to make things right. But that wouldn't happen.

Sorrow expanded inside of her so quickly, sucking the air from her lungs, taking up too much space. A gasp escaped from her as tears welled from her eyes.

Tyler quickly pulled to the side of the road and stopped the car. "I've got you." Her voice cracked as she reached across the center console to hold Layla. "You're going to be okay."

"Oh, Tyler..." Layla fought to catch her breath. Her heart hurt so much, she couldn't find the words to express the pain.

Would she ever be okay again?

Chapter Twenty-Four

Bastian walked down the stairs at his grandmother's house.

The smell of coffee filled the air.

Charlotte was already up. Honestly, he hoped she wouldn't be. That he'd have a moment alone to make a cup of coffee and drink it.

A little over a week had passed since she'd been in the hospital. He'd been trying to look after her, but she was stubborn. All they'd done was mostly argue.

He walked into the kitchen.

Charlotte looked youthful but a bit too thin in black skinny pants and an oversize blue blouse. From the smoothness of her silvery blond bob, the glow of makeup on her face and the smell of perfume lingering as she limped past him, it was obvious where she'd planned to go.

Just a week out of the hospital, and she wouldn't take it easy and rest. Or completely obey Dr. Kyle's instructions about her blood pressure.

That's why he was calling Aaron and telling him he wouldn't take the job. He needed to stay closer to home and look after her.

Charlotte glanced over at him as she took creamer from the refrigerator. "Good morning." She carried the carton to the counter next to the coffeepot, where she poured the dark brew and some creamer into a mug.

"You're supposed to be cutting back on caffeine."

"I need a jumpstart. It's going to be a long day."

"Did you take your blood pressure pills yet?"

"No. I need to eat first. Otherwise, they upset my stomach."

She limped slightly on the way to the table. The cane she refused to use sat propped in the corner on the other side of the kitchen.

When she'd passed out at the store, she'd injured her knee again...because of Layla and her sister.

Hurt pinged in his chest. A sister he didn't know she'd had. Another omitted detail in a long list of them. He shouldn't have gotten involved with her. He should have done a better job of looking after his grandmother's interests. If he had, she wouldn't have gotten hurt again.

Irritation grew inside of him. He snatched up the cane, walked over to Charlotte and propped it against the table. "You need to start using this and paying attention to the rest of the things Dr. Kyle told you."

"You need to stop fussing at me and hurry up and start that job in Virginia."

"I'm not taking the job in Virginia. I'm staying here."

"Oh no, you're not." Ignoring him, she calmly sipped her coffee.

"I've already decided. I'm putting in an application to become a sheriff's deputy."

"Then find somewhere else to live. Because you're not staying here or in my cottage pretending to be happy."

"I won't be pretending. Knowing you're taken care of *will* make me happy, and it would be a whole lot easier if I was staying here."

"No."

"Why?"

"Because you're making the worst mistake of your life." Charlotte plunked her mug down on the table and coffee sloshed over the side. "Ow!"

He quickly reached for her hand. "Let me see. How bad is it?"

"Stop." She pushed him away.

"No. Us butting heads all day is what needs to stop." He snatched the dish towel from the counter and came back to the table. "Why are you fighting me so hard on this along with everything else?"

Charlotte slipped the towel from his grasp. "Sit down. There's something you need to hear."

Great. What was she going to get on him about

now? As Bastian dropped down in the other chair, she wiped up the spill. "I'm listening."

"I called Ruby yesterday."

That was a name he didn't need to hear. "You called her? Why?"

"I wanted to make sure Layla was okay. And I needed to talk to Ruby."

"Is she okay?" The question slipped out before he could stop it.

Charlotte's blue-eyed gaze rested on his face. "You could find out yourself."

He'd been tempted so many times to call Layla. But then he would remember how she lied to him. And how much he'd cared for Layla and wanted to be with her.

"Why would you want to talk to Ruby. What's left to say?"

"I apologized to her."

"Apologized? For what? All she and her family have done is cause trouble in your life."

Charlotte carefully folded the towel and put it on the table. "Riding in the ambulance last week, wondering if I'd see another day, I had an epiphany. I'd wasted too much time holding on to a grudge, and I regretted it.

"After talking to Ruby, we both realize now there was much more going on than a disagreement over opening another shop. We had differing points about a few other things as well. But we never talked about it. The tension between us built up until it exploded into an argument. We attacked each other. We were both hurt about our partnership ending. But to make it easier on ourselves, we made each other the villain in our own stories about what happened."

"So what are you saying? Now we're supposed to give everyone a pass on their screwed-up behavior?"

"Don't do that."

"Do what?"

"Pass judgment. When it comes to what happened with Ruby and I, you can't. You weren't here when the Bee and Tee's partnership ended. When you say everyone, you mean Layla, and in all fairness, you also have to look at what happened with her based on the choices you made, and the ones you didn't."

"Layla hid the truth from me. What else is there to see?"

Actually, there was more to see. He let his guard down around Layla when he shouldn't have. And he couldn't pinpoint when it happened.

Yes, he could.

Standing in the doorway between their rooms at the motel. He'd lost perspective because she'd smiled at him over a bag of pretzels. She'd taken his breath away, and in that moment, he'd wanted to keep making her smile, even if it meant sacrificing the ability to breathe.

Bastian exhaled pent-up disappointment. "I can't trust anything that happened with Layla. I wasn't with the woman I thought I was. I'm not even sure I really knew her."

"Don't you? Layla never pretended to be anything but herself. Kind, generous, a talented dressmaker.

If you'd wanted to know more about her, you could have just looked her up. But you didn't. Why?"

"I don't know." Sitting back, he massaged the tightness in his temples then ran his hands down his face. He needed a shave. He just wanted coffee. He didn't want to talk about Layla, but his gran was insisting. "Maybe I wanted her to be something she could never be, and I just didn't want to see it."

"I think she was exactly what you needed her to be." Charlotte grasped his arm. "When you came back from your interview, you said something I never thought I'd hear you say. You said, 'I'm home.'"

"I was home."

"You've never called Bolan home before. And that's partially my fault. Growing up, Diane always brought you here on the heels of something bad. Being here was never about enjoyment for you. Even now as an adult, you show up to repair things, clean up after bad storms and to take care of me."

"Of course I do those things. I'm your grandson. That's what I should be doing."

"And I'm grateful for all of that, but Bastian, I need you to see the whole picture." As Charlotte leaned in, strength and love were in her eyes. "With Layla you were happy to be here. You smiled more than you ever have. You spent time with friends. Layla did something I could never do. She made this place home."

"Even if she did, it doesn't erase her choices while she was with me."

Charlotte gave him an indulging smile. "You

can debate that all you want. But cutting the people we care about out of our lives because of mistakes that can be fixed, or disagreements that could be resolved, only robs us of something. Time we could have spent with them. I'm sad that I missed all those years with Ruby. If I could go back in time, I would make up with her. And I bet if Layla could go back in time, she would do things differently, too."

If he could go back in time, maybe he never would have stopped that night when he spotted her car on the side of the road. No. He would have. Helping her then was the right choice. But later on... He hadn't thought things through. He normally did. He didn't just leap into things like he had with Layla.

"We can't go back in time, Gran. What's done is done."

"But you can go forward. You can take that job like you're meant to in Virginia. And you can reconsider what the future could hold." She hesitated. "Layla fell in love with you."

"You don't know that."

"She told me, and I believe her. I also know you feel the same way about her, but right now, you'd rather think with your head than listen to your heart." Charlotte leaned in and gently tapped him in the middle of his chest. "But before you decide to cut Layla completely out of your life, make sure that's the choice your heart wants to make. Because if you let Layla go now, and you're wrong, you might not get her back."

* * *

Later that night, Bastian couldn't sleep. The only creatures awake were him and the crickets chirping a symphony outside the cottage.

He got out of bed and pulled on a pair of black shorts. After grabbing his phone off the nightstand, he walked outside onto the front porch.

Dropping down on the top stair, he took in the lawn, trees, and the neighbor's fields bathed in moonlight.

It was perfect nighttime sitting weather. He'd forgotten what this was like. This was something he hadn't done with Layla. But as he sat there, he could easily imagine her sitting beside him with her head on his shoulder.

Was his gran right about her making Bolan more like home for him?

Bastian searched his memory, trying to remember what he did when he came to Bolan as an adult before Layla entered his life.

Just like she'd mentioned, he could recall repairing things. Cleaning up after storms. He'd never attended events. And how many times had Mace invited him out for lunch or a beer back then, and he'd claimed he didn't have time. Plenty.

But with Layla…

A replay of images flashed in his mind of the moments he'd enjoyed with her during their few short weeks together. The things he'd never cared to experience with anyone or made time to do…until her.

Date night at the Starlight Tasting, dancing at

the bar in the Montecito. Breakfast with his grand-mother. Sharing vending machine cuisine on a blanket at the motel. Their in-depth conversation about zombie movies and pretzel dust.

As he thought about those moments, warmth radiated over him. It was as if he could feel Layla's joy. And her absence. The ache in his heart that he'd tried to deny since she'd left grew stronger.

Those moments had been real to him and meaningful. And he'd miss them if they were no longer part of his life. No, not just the moments.

He'd miss Layla.

Chapter Twenty-Five

Sitting on the light beige couch in her living room, Layla took a jumbo pretzel stick out of the bag on her lap. She dipped it into the bowl of cheese sauce sitting on a tray beside her that also had a glass of chardonnay.

It wasn't wise tempting fate by not putting the tray on the coffee table. But the convenience of not having to move very far made living dangerously worth it.

Using the remote, she turned up the volume on the British crime drama playing on the television in front of her.

Tyler had invited her to go out, but she was settling in for a peaceful Friday night. And if she was lucky, Tyler wouldn't bother her until at least Sunday.

Since they'd returned to Atlanta two weeks ago,

Tyler had practically stayed on her hip, checking in almost daily to make sure she was okay.

Kinsley was a close second with a text or a phone call, sometimes both on the same day, at least three times a week.

She loved them both, but she was okay.

Layla took a long sip of wine, washing down the pretzel. Yes, she'd completely fallen apart and cried her eyes out on the beach, but her heart was starting to mend. Sort of. *Zombie Robot Soldier Beasts*, the film Bastian had claimed was a cinematic masterpiece, was on another channel.

She'd started watching it. But instead of falling into the story or laughing at how seriously insane the plot was, she'd started to tear up and had to change the channel.

Would missing Bastian ever stop?

As Layla ate another pretzel stick, her phone, also on the tray, dinged in a text message.

She glanced at the screen. It was from Tyler.

Come to dinner. I have an in for that new restaurant on Peachtree Street. No waiting!

Interesting. One of her clients had recently raved about the restaurant's butter-braised lobster dish. But not even the best lobster dish in town was worth getting up to do her hair, putting on makeup and changing out of her sweats.

Layla put down the pretzel stick she was nibbling

on. After wiping the crumbs from her fingers on her thigh, she picked up her phone and answered.

Shoot! Already had dinner. Have fun.

She put the phone down, picked up her pretzel and dunked it in the cheese sauce.

Another text from Tyler appeared.

Leftovers sound good.

No! Layla licked her fingers. Where was her napkin? Darn it. She texted one-handed.

Keys in the front lock rattled.

Tyler had a key for emergencies. She was going to have to give Tyler another refresher on what *emergency* meant.

The front door opened.

"Hey, I'm here," Tyler called out.

A moment later, she strode into the living room wearing a black-and-white dress, electric-blue stilettos, carrying a fashion portfolio clutch.

She glanced at Layla from her pulled-back hair all the way down to her fuzzy socks.

"Don't say it. I know what I look like."

"I wasn't going to say anything. I was just thinking that it was a good thing we didn't try to make it to the restaurant." She circled her finger in the air as she pointed at Layla. "That would have taken way too long to fix."

"Gee, thanks."

"I'm just kidding. You look cute. Even with cheese sauce on your face."

"Why are you here?" In anticipation of Tyler plopping down on the couch beside her, Layla moved the tray to the coffee table.

"I have good news." Tyler slipped off her shoes. "Is there more wine?"

"In the fridge. Take my glass. I need a refill."

"I'll bring back the bottle." A short time later, Tyler returned with the bottle and her own full wineglass.

Layla held hers up for a refill and Tyler poured. "What's the news?"

Tyler put the bottle on the coffee table and dropped down beside Layla. "The ball has started to roll on the production of my collection and it's going to be fabulous."

"Congrats." Layla clinked wineglasses with her. "I'm really excited for you."

Grandma Ruby had talked to Charlotte and Charlotte had accepted the money. But Grandma Ruby had made up her mind before that, giving Tyler permission to pursue her dream.

"So you gave up reservations at a prime spot to come tell me that?"

"Yes and no." Tyler placed her glass on the coffee table then dug into the clutch. She pulled out an open, square, white linen envelope and handed it to Layla.

"What's this?"

"It's an invite to Eden's wedding. Charlotte sent it to Grandma for you."

"That was nice of her." Layla deposited the envelope on the coffee table. Charlotte probably wanted her to have a souvenir for making the dress.

"There's a note inside of it." Tyler looked between her and the envelope. "Aren't you going to read it?"

"And how would you know about the note? Oh right, the envelope is already open. So why don't you just tell me."

Tyler scooped up the wineglass. "For your information, I didn't open it, Grandma did. Anyway, the note is about the wives' tale of not sewing the last stitch in the wedding dress until immediately before the bride walks down the aisle. Do you remember it? Eden wants you to sew the final stitch for good luck."

"Oh no." Layla waved her off with a pretzel stick. "I'm done with jinxes, curses and superstitions."

"This isn't about any of that. It's symbolic tradition. A harmonious karmic exchange that will make the bride feel that good luck is following her down the aisle as she starts a new chapter in her life. And Grandma Ruby and I both agree it's the beginning of yours."

"What are you talking about?"

"Your future as a designer."

"I said I would *think* about working with you at Sashay Chic. I'm still an accountant."

"But are you happy as an accountant?"

"I am." At least she was most of the time.

"I think you're scared. And I get it—two plus two will always equal four on a spreadsheet. It's not like a fresh page in a sketchbook where there is no guarantee about what might show up on the pages. It's safe. But what is playing safe getting you? Don't you want to keep what you found in Bolan making Eden's dress?"

Escape, peace—she had found those things making Eden's dress. But she'd also found something she hadn't anticipated. Bastian.

Layla swallowed sadness with a sip of wine. But she had to move on, right? "Maybe I'll consider designing part-time or something, but I can't go back to Maryland and sew Eden's dress."

"Because of him?"

The words lodged in her throat. Layla could only nod.

Tyler scooted over and wrapped an arm around her. "I know it's hard, sister of mine, but you will survive. You'll grow strong. And you'll learn how to get along."

"You did not just quote a classic song lyric as a solution." Layla's almost tears dried up in disbelief.

"Song lyrics? No." Tyler laughed a bit too loudly and then her laugh died away. "Wait a minute. Didn't you quote lyrics to me when Jerrold and I broke up before my junior prom? Now that I think about it, you made me sing them with you."

Tyler tossed her hair in dramatic fashion and sang into a fake microphone. "'At first I was afraid, I was petrified.'" She held the fake microphone out to Layla.

"No. I. Didn't…" But a memory from years ago flashed into Layla's mind of the two of them singing at the top of their lungs. And Tyler had stopped crying. "Okay, maybe I did make you sing that song. But you were miserable, and I was desperate. And I was not going to let some boy with a mustache drawn on his top lip stop you from wearing the gorgeous dress you made."

Tyler mocked deep contemplation. "Really? Actually, it's brilliant. Or maybe I'm just brilliant for remembering what you said to me back then so I could drop that knowledge on you now. Boom!"

"Ugh. Do you ever stop?" Layla tried to shove Tyler away, but she clung to her like an octopus.

"No, and I never will, because I love you." Tyler smacked a kiss to Layla's cheek. Sincerity came into her eyes. "But seriously, I'm not making light of what happened with Bastian. I know you still care about him. But if there's no hope for you and him to be together, you have to find closure. And the best place to do that isn't on this couch. It's in Maryland."

Chapter Twenty-Six

Standing in front of the closed doors leading into the church, Eden beamed radiance as the photographer snapped candid shots of her and Layla.

Arranging the skirt of her coral-colored dress, Layla knelt at the hem of Eden's wedding gown.

She reached for the small satin drawstring bag next to her, and as she picked it up, her fingers brushed over the floral, embroidered pattern on the side of it.

The design incorporated her, Tyler's, and their mother's and Grandma Ruby's first initials.

Grandma Ruby and Tyler had given her the bag before she'd left Atlanta. They said it was filled with love and would bring her good fortune. And she needed them. Being back in Maryland, seeing

Charlotte but no signs of Bastian, had raised a mix of emotions.

But now she needed to set them aside and focus on the important task at hand.

Layla loosened the drawstring and the bag flattened out, revealing an assortment of sewing tools.

She removed a needle, scissors and a spool of white thread. "Okay, here we go."

"Thank you for doing this." Eden's smile reflected pure joy that was as luminous as the sparkling tiara on her head. "And thank you for giving me the perfect dress."

"You're welcome. And you're the reason it's perfect. You're beautiful."

As Layla spotted happy tears in Eden's eyes, she felt her own welling up. Mocking sternness, she pointed at Eden. "No crying. You'll ruin your makeup."

"You're right." Laughing, Eden fanned her eyes.

Layla cut the thread and looped it through the needle. She secured the single length of thread on the inside fold of the hem with a small knot.

"Make a small stitch, catching just a few threads of the fabric. Then make a longer stitch on the inside fold…"

Just like in the past, the instructions played in her mind. But this time, her mom's voice was loud and clear, and she remembered when she'd heard it. It was the day her mother had given her the Easter dress. They'd sewn the final stitches in the hem together.

In the present, it was as if she could feel her

mom's guiding hand over hers as she made each stitch in Eden's gown.

And in her mind, she heard something else her mother had said that day. Something she'd forgotten.

"You're so good at this, Layla. Some day, you're going to make beautiful dresses. I can see it in you..."

The remembered love and pride on her mom's face was like a tight hug. She could feel the bond that had existed between Grandma Ruby and her mom. She was part of it, too.

Tears started to fill Layla's eyes. *You were right, Mom. I'm doing it.*

The journey of making Eden's dress had brought doubt, triumph and, unfortunately, heartbreak. But it had set her on a path for her life. One that her mom had known all those years ago was right. And now she finally saw it, too.

Managing her emotions, Layla made the last stitch then cut and knotted the thread. "It's finished."

One of the wedding planning crew spoke into her headset. "Two-minute warning. The bride is on her way." As the woman handed Eden an exquisite cascade made with long-stemmed calla lilies, she gave Layla a polite smile. "Take your seat, please. The bride has to go in last."

Layla gathered up her sewing bag then grabbed her purse from a nearby bench along the wall. As she hurried to the side door, the heels of her stilettos thumped on the carpet. Before she went in, she quickly tucked away the bag in her purse.

Inside the packed church, Layla spotted Charlotte

on the end of the second pew from the back with an open space beside her. They were each other's plus-one for the wedding.

Having flown in late last night, she'd gone straight to Tillbridge Guesthouse to check in and hadn't seen Charlotte since that morning outside the church. Their reunion had been poignant but brief. They'd have plenty of time to talk after the ceremony.

Layla zipped her purse as she reached the pew.

Smiling, Charlotte looked up and stood.

The man on the other side of the space stood, too.

Bastian...

Surprise weakened Layla's legs and she dropped down right away.

Whispering, Charlotte nudged her. "Move over."

As Layla scooted closer to Bastian, his gaze stayed on her face. She looked away. But not before getting a good glimpse of him. His hair was cut in a military-style fade. Clean-shaven and wearing a navy suit and tie with a snowy white shirt, he was nothing short of gorgeous.

Moments later, the organist played the opening flourish of notes for the bridal chorus, and everyone came to their feet as Eden met her groom at the altar.

As they sat back down, Layla's leg pressed against Bastian's. With Charlotte on the other side of her, she couldn't move.

Suffused in a rush of prickling heat, her dress suddenly felt like it was made of two-inch-thick wool instead of lightweight satin.

If she'd known he was going to be there, she

would have… What? Not come to the ceremony? No, she still would have come, but she would have been better prepared. She'd already envisioned running into the couples' night crew, anticipating awkward hellos and pasting a bright smile on her face. But seeing Bastian—what was the game plan for running into the guy you loved when he wanted nothing to do with you? Did one even exist?

"Just go…" Those had been his last words to her, and he'd meant them.

Memories of being with him from the day he'd driven up on the side of the road and offered to pull her out of the ditch to the day she'd disappointed him replaced the present ceremony in front of her.

Bittersweetness swam inside of her.

Mendelssohn's "Wedding March" reverberated through the church as the newly hitched bride and groom, along with the bridal party and family, exited the church.

Charlotte stood, her demeanor as placid as her smile. "That was a lovely service. Bastian, why don't you show Layla the meditation garden? You remember where it is, don't you? And don't worry about me getting to the reception. I'm catching a ride with a friend." She walked away.

With people waiting for her to exit the pew, Layla merged with guests, filing out of the open side doors. It sounded like Charlotte was working from her own script of events. Had she left Bastian in the dark about her coming back to town?

In the foyer, only guests remained, chatting with each other.

The wedding planners had already spirited away the wedding party and families of the bride and groom. Guests greeting the newlyweds would take place at the reception in an hour.

As Layla slung her thin purse strap over her shoulder, Bastian's light touch to her elbow made her jump in surprise.

He pointed to an exit just down the hall. "The garden is that way."

Layla almost said no. But they hadn't talked since Charlotte's panic attack. Maybe this was a chance for real closure.

Outside the door, they walked down a path lined with an array of colorful flowers, trees and budding bushes. The light, sweet scent of nearby roses drifted in the air along with the scents of green grass and rich soil.

They paused.

Wanting to get it over with, like pulling off a Band-Aid, Layla went in first. "I'm sensing Charlotte just sprung this on you. I didn't know you would be here."

"No, she didn't tell me you'd be here. She just said she needed a plus-one for the ceremony."

"She told me I was her plus-one."

Bastian chuckled softly. "Yeah, that sounds like something Gran would do. But I suspected she was up to something."

"And you came anyway?" Curiosity pushed out

the question, but she hadn't meant to say it. "You don't have to answer that."

"I know, but I will. I wanted to see you."

"Why?"

As he looked away, his face remained unreadable.

Why had she asked him that? She might not be ready for the answer. Dread swirled in her stomach as she prepared for him to say the worst or maybe not answer at all.

"Because I shouldn't have ended things the way I did at the hospital. I should have listened to what you had to say."

"I should have told you sooner. I'm sorry."

"Why didn't you?"

Layla had mulled through the answer enough times in her head, but she'd never said it aloud. "I had a plan. Give Charlotte the money and leave. But things got complicated. I never expected to have to design a wedding dress or end up working at Buttons & Lace. Or that I would enjoy it all so much."

It was so easy to stop right there. To save herself from rejection or disbelief. But she had to tell him. Layla dropped her gaze. "And most of all, I didn't anticipate meeting you. I just wanted what we had to keep going. I didn't want us to end. That's why I hesitated."

"I didn't want things to end either." As Bastian took hold of her hand, her heart bumped in her chest. "My mom had a history of making excuses after the fact. I just assumed that's what you were going to do. It was easier to push you away than risk being disappointed."

She looked up at him. "But I did disappoint you."

He tugged her closer. "Not in the same way. I wish you would have told me you were Ruby's granddaughter. It hurt that after we got close, you didn't trust me enough to tell me. But I made choices, too. I accepted that you didn't want to dive too deeply into your personal life. And that implied I wouldn't judge you unfairly. But I did. And I'm sorry for that."

A light breeze blew over them, taking away some of the heaviness she'd felt. "I wish I could go back and do it all differently."

"Me, too. Unfortunately, we can't. But there is one thing we can do."

"Forgive ourselves?"

"That, too. We can also start over." He let go of her hand then extended one of his. "Hello, I'm Sebastian Raynes. But most people call me Bastian."

His small smile prompted her to play along. "Hi, I'm Layla Price."

They shook hands, but he held on to hers and frowned. "So how long do you think we should wait before we get to the kissing stage?"

"I have no idea what the rules are. Maybe weeks."

"Oh hell no. I can't wait that long." Bastian pulled her closer, took her by the waist and pressed his mouth to hers.

Forgiveness and a new beginning never tasted so sweet.

A long moment later, they came up for air.

He laid his forehead to hers. "Okay, so maybe we're going to move through the steps of this do-over a little faster than anticipated."

"We can." As she looked up at him, she rested her hands on his chest. "As long as in between the kissing, we're having lots of honest conversation."

He smiled. "I can live with that."

As she lifted on her toes to press her mouth to his, Layla's phone rang with a familiar ring chime.

Tyler...

Bastian glanced down at her purse. "Do you need to get that?"

"No. It's just my sister. She can wait." She'd catch Tyler up later. Layla wound her arms around Bastian's neck and joined him for a kiss.

Returning to Bolan had been all about good karma. She'd not only stitched up the wedding dress. She had also mended her heart.

Chapter Twenty-Seven

Ten months later...

Ruby pointed to the image on the sketch pad in front of her and Charlotte where they huddled over it on the worktable. "The lace on the bodice needs to extend down a bit more."

"Maybe..." Charlotte shook her head with a pensive frown. "But if we take it too far down on the sides, it will interfere with the shape of the skirt."

"True. But that skirt... It needs something."

Both women cocked their heads to the side, contemplating the design they'd been working on all morning.

Layla, standing off to the side near the doorway, couldn't stop a smile. The collaboration bug had bitten Charlotte and Ruby. Since the two women's reunion, they'd met up several times over the past months in Atlanta and Bolan to discuss new designs.

Suffering from a bit of fatigue after arriving late last night, Layla turned to leave, planning to satisfy her caffeine craving.

"Wait," Ruby called out to Layla. "We need another opinion on this skirt."

Layla hesitated. A request for one opinion usually led to two or ten. And if that happened, she'd never make it to the kitchen for a cup of coffee. "It sounds like you ladies have it covered. Really. It looks great."

The two women pinned her with an obey-your-elders stare, and Layla joined them.

Charlotte glanced between Layla and the drawing. "What do you think?"

"Another wedding dress? Are you working on a line of bridal gowns?"

"No." Ruby shrugged. "We're just doodling."

"So what do you think?" Charlotte's brow rose with a smile. "Would you wear it?"

Both women's facial expressions remained innocent, but the project the two were collaborating on was obvious.

Layla turned her attention to the sketch.

The gown had a delicate-looking lace bodice and a sheer, full skirt. She would feel happy wearing the dress. Especially if Bastian was waiting for her at the altar.

Layla allowed herself a moment to savor the image and smiled. Someday.

Bastian had a busy schedule, working for Max-Pointe. Currently, he was out of the country. She missed him. But she also understood. He was in his dream job, and she was embracing hers.

She was splitting her time between creating a specialty clothing line with Tyler for Sashay Chic and helping Charlotte update the business plan for Buttons & Lace. And she was handling the store's financials.

But the part that made her smile the most. She and Bastian were figuring it out and making the long-distance arrangement work for them as a couple.

"It's beautiful." Layla pointed to the drawing. "With the fullness of the skirt, could you add pockets without destroying the lines of the dress?"

"We absolutely could." Charlotte quickly added them to the sketch.

"Perfect." Ruby beamed. "Just the thing a modern bride needs."

As the two women went back into their own creative bubble, Layla backed out of the room. Coffee and a long walk. That's what—

As she turned to walk down the hallway, she ran into a wall—a human one. Recognition turned a low shriek of surprise into one of happiness. "Bastian!" As he grasped her waist, she pressed her mouth to his, reveling in a long kiss.

"What are you doing here?" she murmured against his lips. "I thought you were traveling with a client to Italy."

His mouth curved into a smile against hers. "We came back early."

Bastian deepened the kiss, and as she molded herself to him, desire sped up her heart rate.

Charlotte's and Ruby's cackles drifting from the other room filtered into her thoughts.

She leaned away from him. "You should probably say hello to them."

"In a minute," he whispered, squeezing her waist. "It was a long flight. Let me grab a cup of coffee first."

She whispered back, "No argument from me."

Smiling at each other as if they were getting away with the caper of the century, they held hands, creeping down the hall, and went down the stairs.

Entering the kitchen, she gave in to the desire to kiss him again.

As she sank into him, Bastian caressed up and down her back. He eased out of the kiss. "I missed you."

"I missed you, too." Just as she went to slip her arms around his neck, Bastian moved away.

"I dreamed about café-mocha-flavored coffee on the plane. I hope Gran has some." He walked into the corner pantry. "Damn—I don't see any."

"Check the top shelf."

"Found it," he called out. "And she's got peach jam. Perfect. I brought croissants from Brewed Haven. They're in the refrigerator. Can you heat a couple up in the microwave for us?"

"Okay. I'm surprised the box of croissants made

it home. You're so addicted to them, sometimes I almost wonder if you love them more than me." Laughing, Layla opened the refrigerator.

The ring with a marquise diamond winking at her from a small blue jewelry box on the middle shelf stole a breath from her.

Bastian walked out of the pantry. "I could never love anything or anyone more than I love you."

Awestruck by surprise, she stared at him, unable to speak.

He took the box out of the refrigerator and removed the ring.

"Oh…" Soft emotions overcame her as he took a knee.

"Layla, will you marry me?"

Movement in the kitchen archway caught her attention.

Charlotte and Ruby stood together, holding hands with all the hope in the world written on their faces.

Layla looked to Bastian. All she felt for him welled inside of her and she saw the same in his eyes. "Yes."

As Bastian slipped the ring on her finger, Charlotte and Ruby spoke to someone on speakerphone. "She said yes!"

Cheers erupted over the phone line.

Bastian stood and took her by the waist. "That's your family."

"I guessed that."

As she slid her arms up and around his neck, Bastian stared into her eyes. "I love you, Layla."

The same rush she'd felt the first time Bastian had said her name came over her as pure joy filled her heart. "I love you, too."

He kissed her, and something just as powerful as love enveloped her. A certainty about their destiny together and what awaited them—happiness until the end of time.

* * * * *

Don't miss the first book in the
Small Town Secrets miniseries

The Chef's Kiss

Available now wherever Harlequin Special Edition
books and ebooks are sold!

#2935 THE MAVERICK'S MARRIAGE PACT
Montana Mavericks: Brothers & Broncos • by Stella Bagwell

To win an inheritance, Maddox John needs to get married as quickly as possible. But can he find a woman to marry him for all the wrong reasons?

#2936 THE RIVALS OF CASPER ROAD
Garnet Run • by Roan Parrish

When heartbroken Bram Larkspur finds out the street he's just moved onto has a Halloween decorating contest, he thinks it's a great way to meet people. He isn't expecting to meet Zachary Glass, the buttoned-up architect across the street who resents having competition...and whom he's quickly falling for.

#2937 LONDON CALLING
The Friendship Chronicles • by Darby Baham

Robin Johnson has just moved to London after successfully campaigning for a promotion at her job and is in search of a new adventure and love. After several misfires, she finally meets a guy she is attracted to and feels safe with, but can she really give him a chance?

#2938 THE COWGIRL AND THE COUNTRY M.D.
Top Dog Dude Ranch • by Catherine Mann

Dr. Nolan Barnett just gained custody of his two orphaned grandchildren and takes them to the Top Dog Dude Ranch to bond, only to be distracted by the pretty stable manager. Eliza Hubbard just landed her dream job and must focus. However, they soon find the four of them together feels a lot like a family.

#2939 THE MARINE'S CHRISTMAS WISH
The Brands of Montana • by Joanna Sims

Marine captain Noah Brand is temporarily on leave to figure out if his missing ex-girlfriend's daughter is his—and he needs his best friend Shayna Wade's help. Will this Christmas open his eyes to the woman who's been there this whole time?

#2940 HER GOOD-LUCK CHARM
Lucky Stars • by Elizabeth Bevarly

Rory's amnesia makes her reluctant to get close to anyone, including sexy neighbor Felix. But when it becomes clear he's the key to her memory recovery, they have no choice but to stick very close together.

HSECNM0822

*When heartbroken Bram Larkspur finds out the street
he's just moved onto has a Halloween decorating
contest, he thinks it's a great way to meet people.
He isn't expecting to meet Zachary Glass, the
buttoned-up architect across the street who resents
having competition...and whom he's quickly falling for.*

Read on for a sneak peek at
The Rivals of Casper Road,
the latest in Roan Parrish's Garnet Run series!

He opened the mailbox absently and reached inside.
There should be an issue of *Global Architecture*. But the
moment the mailbox opened, something hit him in the
face. Shocked, he reeled backward. Had a bomb gone
off? Had the world finally ended?

He sputtered and opened his eyes. His mailbox,
the ground around it and presumably he himself were
covered in...glitter?

"What the...?"

"Game on," said a voice over his shoulder, and Zachary
turned to see Bram standing there, grinning.

"You— I— Did you—?"

"You started it," Bram said, nodding toward the
dragon. "But now it's on."

Zachary goggled. Bram had seen him. He'd seen him do something mean-spirited and awful, and had seen it in the context of a prank... He was either very generous or very deluded. And for some reason, Zachary found himself hoping it was the former.

"I'm very, very sorry about the paint. I honestly don't know what possessed me. That is, I wasn't actually possessed. I take responsibility for my actions. Just, I didn't actually think I was going to do it until I did, and then, uh, it was too late. Because I'd done it."

"Yeah, that's usually how that works," Bram agreed. But he still didn't seem angry. He seemed...impish.

"Are you...enjoying this?"

Bram just raised his eyebrows and winked. "Consider us even. For now." Then he took a magazine from his back pocket and handed it to Zachary. *Global Architecture.*

"Thanks."

Bram smiled mysteriously and said, "You never know what I might do next." Then he sauntered back across the street, leaving Zachary a mess of uncertainty and glitter.

HARLEQUIN
PLUS

Announcing a **BRAND-NEW** multimedia subscription service for romance fans like you!

Read, Watch and Play.

Experience the easiest way to get the romance content you crave.

Start your **FREE 7 DAY TRIAL** at <u>www.harlequinplus.com/freetrial</u>.